About the Author

JANET AYLMER is the pen name of an English Jane Austen enthusiast who lives in Bath.

Darcy's Story

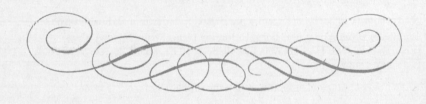

JANET AYLMER

HARPER

NEW YORK · LONDON · TORONTO · SYDNEY

HARPER

A previous edition of this book was published in Great Britain in 1996 by Copperfield Books.

FIRST HARPER PAPERBACK PUBLISHED 2006.

Designed by Jaime Putorti

Library of Congress Cataloging-in-Publication Data

Aylmer, Janet.
    Darcy's story/Janet Aylmer.—1st ed.
      p.cm.
    Pride and prejudice retold from Mr. Darcy's perspective.
    ISBN-10: 0-06-114870-9
    ISBN-13: 978-0-06-114870-5
    1. Social classes—Fiction. 2. Courtship—Fiction. 3. England—
Fiction. I. Austen, Jane, 1775–1817. Pride and prejudice. II. Title

    PR6101.Y46D37 2006
    813'.6—dc22

                         2006041216

06 07 08 09 10 ❖/RRD 10 9 8 7 6 5

This book is dedicated to the very many people who have enjoyed reading Pride and Prejudice since it was first published in 1813, and especially to

Rachel

Who always wants to know more.

Preface

Jane Austen's famous novel *Pride and Prejudice* was first published in 1813, and it has been popular with readers ever since.

In Elizabeth Bennet and Fitzwilliam Darcy, she created two of the best loved characters in romantic fiction. Millions of people over the years have been intrigued by Mr. Darcy, the handsome, proud but enigmatic hero of the novel, and the story of how he meets, misunderstands and finally is united with Elizabeth Bennet.

However, *Pride and Prejudice* reveals surprisingly little about Darcy and how he is changed from a *"haughty, reserved and fastidious"* young man to the ardent and humble suitor for the hand of the woman he loves.

Darcy's Story explores Darcy's thoughts and actions, and the reasons behind them, and demonstrates that the hero is just as interesting a person as Elizabeth Bennet herself.

Many readers of the novel have agreed with the author when she described Elizabeth Bennet in a letter to her sister

Cassandra as being "as delightful a creature as ever appeared in print." Her independence of mind, and lack of respect for people who take their social position too seriously, have been described as very modern for the time, now nearly two centuries ago, when the book was completed.

Darcy is a more sombre and reserved personality than Elizabeth, very conscious of his social position, and often appearing aloof and distant. In the story, he observes himself that *"my temper would perhaps be called resentful."* Described by the author of *Pride and Prejudice* early in the book as *"the proudest, most disagreeable man in the world,"* Darcy changes so much that Elizabeth can assure her father that *"Indeed he has no improper pride. He is perfectly amiable. You do not know what he really is . . ."*

This book explains much more about Darcy's relationships with his formidable aunt, the forthright Lady Catherine de Bourgh, with his sister, Georgiana, and with his cousin, Colonel Fitzwilliam. We see Elizabeth Bennet, her parents and sisters, and Mr. Bennet's cousin, the odious but comical curate Mr. Collins, through Darcy's eyes.

Darcy's Story reveals how he overcomes the problems and misunderstandings that threaten to separate him from Elizabeth, so that he is able to say to her towards the end of the story *"By you I was properly humbled. I came to you without a doubt of my reception. You shewed me how insufficient were all my pretensions to please a woman worthy of being pleased."*

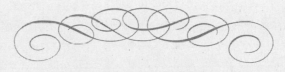

Part One

Mr. Darcy . . . had a fine tall person, handsome features, noble mien . . . and ten thousand pounds a year, but not all his large estate in Derbyshire could save him from being proud, above his company and above being pleased.

1

It is a consequence of possessing an income of ten thousand pounds a year that a man may order his life to his own liking, and choose his own society.

The tall and handsome young man surveying his estate from the first floor window had much to be proud of, and few matters to regret. The estate at Pemberley was ten miles round. The gracious prospect from the house overlooked a verdant valley where the stream had been dammed to form a lake in the foreground. The vista over the park extended across to the woods beyond, where the view widened and the slopes on the far side blended with the trees across the hills to each side. Beyond, the High Peak could be seen in the distance. It was a view of which its owner never wearied; and one of many reasons why he was happier in Derbyshire than in any other place.

"You never tire of that view, Darcy?" said Colonel Fitzwilliam.

"No," he replied, turning to look at his cousin, "but should I?"

"I do not value the landscape of Derbyshire as highly as you do, perhaps, but I dare say that if I had inherited such a handsome house and a fine estate myself, I might have the same preference."

Darcy smiled and answered, "All you lack is a wealthy wife; make a prudent marriage, and you could be in the same position."

His cousin paused for a few moments before saying, "I do not need an heiress to a great estate, just someone whose fortune would compensate for my being the younger son, rather than having the prospect of being the next Earl ___. And I myself give some priority to the lady being agreeable, as you should."

Darcy made no reply to this, but gazed at the prospect over the lake for some time. Then he turned to Fitzwilliam. "Seeing the new growth on the trees at this time of year reminds me that both my mother and later my father died in this month." He paused, and then added, "I am glad to have your company for a few days, for I find it easy to become melancholy in May, indeed resentful that my mother was taken from me so early."

Fitzwilliam reflected it was a very great pity that the late Mr. George Darcy had also not lived longer.

"Your parents were very fond of each other," said Fitzwilliam.

"Yes," said Darcy, "indeed, a rarity in our level of society, I am sure you would agree?"

"You are thinking of Lady Catherine, our aunt, and Sir Lewis de Bourgh, I suppose?"

"They are but one example," said his cousin.

"But do not forget," said Fitzwilliam, "that your mother was very young at the time of her marriage, so that her disposition was not set, whereas our aunt was not only the elder sister, but was two and thirty when she wed. In any case, her marriage was not so much unhappy as more formal. And you should recall that Sir Lewis was an elderly widower when they met, and died only three years later, when his daughter was only two years old. At least his will left Lady Catherine a considerable fortune, together with a very handsome house and with the estate at Rosings in trust for our cousin Anne."

"But if you are trying to suggest," said Darcy testily, "that a gentleman whom our aunt had met taking the waters at Bath, and who was very nearly a contemporary of our grandfather, could have had a really happy marriage with someone of such strong opinions as Lady Catherine, I do not believe you!"

Fitzwilliam reflected to himself that Lady Catherine could more properly be described as arrogant, with an ill concealed contempt for her inferiors in society. Indeed, he knew that Darcy himself could appear to be disdainful in company. Although he had inherited his father's shy, reserved disposition and dislike of the social round in town, in many other respects his cousin strongly resembled his mother, having a strong sense of his social position and being jealous of his ancestry and the possession of his great estate.

"Perhaps it would have been as useful if Sir Lewis could have bequeathed Anne better health rather than so large a fortune, for she was a sickly child from the beginning," said Fitzwilliam. "But you must excuse me, for I must make preparations for when we leave tomorrow."

❅   ❅   ❅

Darcy returned to sit at the table where he had been writing a letter to Georgiana.

His sister, more than ten years his junior, had been left on their father's death five years earlier to the guardianship of himself and his cousin Fitzwilliam. Although she was happiest when in Derbyshire, since their bereavement Georgiana had lived mainly in London, so that she might have access to the best of tutors, and be instructed in music and dancing prior to her being presented at court.

She was now some fifteen years of age, and had lately left school. Darcy had recently employed a Mrs. Younge as his sister's companion, who had been recommended by an acquaintance of his uncle, the Earl ___, for whom she had occupied a similar post. At the suggestion of Mrs. Younge, who knew the place well, she and Georgiana were shortly to travel from Darcy's house in London to Ramsgate, to take the sea air for a few weeks.

They were to break their journey at Rosings, the home of Lady Catherine de Bourgh and her daughter Anne, who was several years' younger than Darcy. He himself had recently spent a few days with Fitzwilliam there on his annual visit, but with little enjoyment from the company of his aunt and cousin.

On Lady Catherine's insistence, Georgiana and Mrs. Younge were to be accompanied on their journey through Kent by a pair of manservants, in addition to the coachman and his assistant, as outriders alongside the chaise.

He took up the letter that he had most recently received from his sister.

I know, my dear brother, that you wish us to visit my aunt on our journey. I confess that lately I find her man-

ner rather severe for my taste, and her strictures on my accomplishments compared to those of Anne rather dispiriting.

Here he paused.

His recollection was that, despite the little time she spent in society, their cousin's health had not enabled her to acquire many accomplishments, save a very proper disdain for inferior companions and a rather constant concern for her own indispositions.

Certainly, any talents Anne might possess were far inferior to those of his sister, although Georgiana was several years younger. However, he was aware that his aunt considered those accomplishments that her daughter lacked would be well within her abilities, should her health ever permit her to acquire them.

"Mrs. Younge tells me that there will be company enough for me in Ramsgate—someone whom we know well from Derbyshire.

I will write to you in London once we have arrived.

Your loving sister,

Georgiana"

Darcy wondered who the someone from Derbyshire could be, as he was not aware of any friend who might be in Kent at present. For a moment, he thought to add to his reply, to mention that he might have time from his business in town to join them for a few days.

However, that was not certain, so he left his letter as it was.

❈   ❈   ❈

The family at Pemberley was well respected in the neighbourhood and, although properly conscious of his position as one of the wealthiest men in the country, the late Mr. George Darcy had been a conscientious employer and benevolent to the poor. Fitzwilliam Darcy had continued his father's habit of giving charity to the deserving without seeking to have it known, as well as Mr. George Darcy's interest in the fine library at Pemberley.

It was during one of his rare visits to London to consult his attorney that George Darcy had met his wife, Lady Anne, daughter of the late Earl ___, in her first season. Her family had considered a marriage to the owner of one of the richest estates in the country eminently suitable for their younger daughter.

George and Lady Anne Darcy had had little in common with their sister in Kent, save considerable wealth and position. However, they were both aware of their family responsibilities. Although Mr. George Darcy had rarely made the journey when he visited town, Lady Anne had been to Rosings regularly.

Before his mother's premature demise, when his sister Georgiana was but a small child, Darcy had gone with them both to stay with Lady Catherine several times a year. Lady Anne's death had been a severe blow to him, leaving him with no close confidant but his cousin Fitzwilliam. Since that unhappy event, Darcy had reduced his attendance on his aunt to one annual visit, and usually went to stay in Kent in the Spring, a few weeks after Easter.

When the weather was inclement, there was little entertainment at Rosings, and Lady Catherine could be a demanding companion. For that reason, Darcy often asked Fitzwilliam to go with him, to provide some relief to his aunt's strictures, and offer more congenial company.

Lady Catherine's opportunities to travel to Pemberley were restricted by her daughter Anne's ill-health and the distance to Derbyshire from Kent. She did, however, make regular visits to the spa at Bath in the hope of improving her daughter's condition, staying with an elderly relative who had a spacious house just off Laura Place.

Wherever she was, she took it upon herself to supervise her nephew and niece from a distance, by writing regularly to advise them on their conduct, their choice of companions, and the limited number of families with whom it was proper for them to associate.

From her most recent communications, Darcy understood that Lady Catherine considered the time was approaching when he should consider marriage. She had hinted strongly that she had one particular lady in mind, that she and her sister had agreed many years ago that this marriage should be made within the family, and to her daughter Anne.

To this idea he was indifferent. At six years and twenty, Darcy was in no hurry to marry.

On leaving the university, Darcy had very soon discovered that young ladies of consequence and of marriageable age were more than happy to be in his company, and that their mothers did their best to entice him to accept social invitations and to put their daughters in his way.

He, however, disliked the season and as far as he could avoided attendance at the social functions in London. He was equally disinclined to attend formal balls and dances at home in Derbyshire, or elsewhere in the country where his friends resided. In any case, he had yet to meet any young woman who took his interest.

He doubted that he would be as fortunate as his father, in finding in his marriage both a person of equal social position (a paramount consideration), and whom he could also regard with the affection that had so manifestly subsisted between his parents. That combination was, as Darcy had noted too often, unlikely to be attained by most people of his own status and fortune.

However, he did agree with his aunt, Lady Catherine, that his future wife must above all be from a family of background and repute equal to his own, as one of the richest men of consequence in the country.

2

After luncheon, the two young men walked through the house. The sight of a miniature on the wall prompted Fitzwilliam to ask Darcy a question.

"I am surprised that you keep an image of that gentleman. I thought that your fears about his disposition had proved to be justified?"

"Yes," replied Darcy, "but this room has been left as it was when my father died, in respect for his memory. In any case, George Wickham's father was a faithful servant to mine, and very kind to me also. He devoted most of his life to running this estate."

"A pity," his cousin replied, "that he did not take more care in his marriage, for his wife was not only much younger, but was also a woman of very extravagant habits, and with a frivolous disposition."

Darcy did not reply.

"I have also heard," said Fitzwilliam, "that George Wickham has been putting it about that you did not discharge your responsibilities to him in accordance with your father's wishes."

"Yes," said Darcy shortly, "but, as you know, there is no truth in that. I hope never to have any more dealings with that gentleman. Hopefully, when I paid him off, that was the end of it."

His cousin's remark reminded Darcy that young Mr. Wickham had been born within a few months of himself. The owner of Pemberley had gladly consented to be godfather to the child of his steward, who was named after him. The boy had been a great favourite of Mr. Darcy, to the extent that his own son had sometimes been jealous of young George Wickham's pleasing address, good figure and very happy readiness of conversation.

The cost of sending the steward's son to school and later to Cambridge had been borne by his godfather. When they were young, the two boys had been regular companions. However, his own acquaintance with the son as he grew to manhood had convinced Darcy that young Mr. Wickham had not inherited the integrity or abilities that had served his father so well. At college, Darcy saw the young man turn to frivolous and dissolute habits, of which his benefactor had remained unaware.

When Darcy's father died, he had asked in his will that provision be made for George Wickham. If the young man desired to take holy orders, the request was that a valuable family living should be his. Mr. George Darcy also left his godson the sum of one thousand pounds.

The steward had not long survived his master. Within

half a year of leaving Cambridge, young Mr. Wickham decided against holy orders and accepted instead the sum of three thousand pounds from Darcy, saying that he intended to study for the law.

Darcy had doubted the likelihood of Wickham applying himself to that profession. He had heard nothing more of his childhood companion, since the day several years ago when the sum of money agreed had been paid to him, until Wickham had written to him when the living at Kympton on the Pemberley estate had become vacant. He said that he had spent the money paid to him, that he had changed his mind, and would now like to go into the Church. He had asked for the living, which included an excellent parsonage house.

Darcy had not deigned to reply himself, but had instructed his attorney to write, saying that all Mr. George Darcy's intentions had been met by paying Wickham a much larger sum than that mentioned in the will.

The living at Kympton was then given to a worthy young man already known to the Darcy family, who appeared to have a true vocation for the Church.

On the morrow, Darcy left his instructions for the estate and the house for the next few weeks with his steward and with Mrs. Reynolds, the housekeeper at Pemberley, who had been with the family since he was a child. He then left in the chaise with Fitzwilliam. After the first day's travel, he said farewell to his cousin, who left to take the stage to Essex to see his family near Chelmsford.

On Darcy's arrival in town, he did not find a letter waiting for him from his sister as he had hoped. Instead, there was a note from his friend Charles Bingley, saying that he had been detained in Scarborough where his sisters were residing for a few weeks. However, he wrote that he should be in town within a few days, staying with his brother-in-law, Mr. Hurst, whose house was but a short walk from Darcy's mansion in the Square.

They had become friends whilst at Cambridge, and Darcy had introduced the younger man to his father, who had enjoyed the company of Bingley on the few occasions they had met before the death of Mr. George Darcy. An easy going, good-looking young man now of some three and twenty years, Bingley came from a respectable family in the north of England. Although the fortune had come from trade, he had inherited property amounting to nearly an hundred thousand pounds from his father. He enjoyed country pursuits and, on leaving the University, had considered purchasing an estate, or at least taking a lease of a property. So far, he had not been able to find a place to his liking.

Bingley was as easily pleased by female company as his friend Darcy was not. He was often in love, but as quickly changed his mind. He had easy, unaffected manners, and was always happy to defer to the superior understanding and judgement of his friend on any topic. After the death of his father, Darcy had been glad of the company of his friend, since at that time his sister, Georgiana, had been but ten years old and away at school.

Bingley had two older sisters. The elder, Louisa, had married Mr. Hurst some years earlier, a man more of fashion than fortune with a house in town in Grosvenor Street. The younger, Miss Caroline Bingley, was a little older than Darcy and of an age when many of her contemporaries were now married. Each had a fortune of twenty thousand pounds.

Darcy was regularly in the company of the two sisters when they were with their brother, and found their concern for their place in society, and their habit of associating only with people of rank, very proper. Both sisters were very fine ladies, although seen by their inferiors as proud and conceited.

The following afternoon, Darcy visited his attorney, Mr. Stone, to discuss his business affairs. On his return, he found a letter waiting for him from Georgiana.

He took his favourite seat in the drawing room, facing the window onto the Square, and began to read.

My dear brother,

We called in at Rosings as I promised.

Our cousin Anne was unwell, and kept to her room. However, Mrs. Younge and I took luncheon with Lady Catherine before continuing on our journey. Our aunt had messages for you that I will pass on when we next meet.

Mrs. Younge and I are now well settled in our lodgings, and Ramsgate is a most delightful place.

We are walking every day along the front by the sea to watch the ebb and flow of the tides. We have also taken a carriage out into the country; there are many pretty lanes and woods to see round about.

I am very much enjoying the opportunity to renew my acquaintance with the gentleman whom I mentioned to you in my last letter. He knows Mrs. Younge quite well, and is just as delightful a companion as I remember him.

He says that I should not tell you anything of his being here, which seems to me a little strange. I have not

*seen him for more than 5 years, when he returned to
Pemberley with you while you were both at Cambridge.*

*If I say that his name begins with W, I shall not be
breaking my promise to him to keep our secret.*

*Your loving sister
Georgiana.*

Darcy read the letter twice through.

Suddenly, a terrible thought came to him. He leapt to his
feet and called to his man to pack an overnight bag, and get
the carriage to the door within half an hour.

3

The journey to Ramsgate seemed to take an unconscionable time. The carriage passed within a few miles of his aunt's home at Rosings, but Darcy was in no mood to pause. He urged the coachman on, but the recent rain had made the going difficult, and it was late in the evening before he reached Ramsgate, and secured a room at the Inn in the main square. Before retiring for the night, he sent his coachman to search out where his sister's lodgings were situated, and told him to report early the following day.

On his calling at the rooms on the next morning after breakfast, Georgiana had been surprised but delighted to see him.

Mrs. Younge's enthusiasm had been much more muted.

Darcy soon found out why in private conversation with his sister. On questioning her as gently as he could, she had confirmed to him that the visitor she had been seeing was Mr. Wickham, whom she had recalled fondly from her childhood acquaintance. After a little further discourse with her brother, Georgiana had confessed that she thought that she was in love, and they were planning to elope together. A carriage to Scotland was already ordered by Wickham for the following morning.

Darcy lost no time. He was directed to where Wickham was staying, a few streets away, and found him making preparation for leaving the next day.

Wickham had always had, in Darcy's recollection, the ability to turn any situation to his own advantage, and he sought to do so now.

"Why, Darcy," he said, "this is a most pleasant surprise, for I did not know that you were planning a visit to Ramsgate. Is this a part of the country with which you are familiar? I had thought that you were away in the north just now."

"So my sister tells me!" said Darcy, since he did not wish to prolong the interview.

Wickham had the grace to look a little discomforted, but said, "She has become a very charming young lady. I have been enjoying her company, as she may have told you."

Darcy had to admire his confidence, but said only "Or is it her fortune that you seek to enjoy?"

"You always assume the worst of me, do you not, Darcy?"

"I have good reason to do so, and certainly on this occasion. Georgiana is but fifteen years' old, and yet you were planning to marry her without the consent of either of her guardians!"

And Darcy told him to leave Ramsgate immediately, to cease all and every communication with Georgiana, and never to contact her again.

"And should you think of making any aspect of this affair public, I will ensure that the circumstances are known wherever in society you choose to impose yourself."

He knew that even Wickham's charm and ease of conversing would not preserve some remnant of his reputation in polite society if the truth were to become generally known. But that would also damage Georgiana, and therefore such public exposure was to be avoided if at all possible.

Wickham left the town that day, leaving Darcy to deal with Mrs. Younge.

The interview with that lady was painful but also of short duration, Darcy making it quite clear that she had betrayed his trust, and that she was immediately discharged from his service.

After she had left the house, Darcy went up to see Georgiana. He told her as little as he could about Wickham's dissolute ways, but did explain that, whatever arts might have been used to gain her affections, the young man had been much more interested in his sister's fortune of thirty thousand pounds than in any else that he might have suggested.

Georgiana took this news with great distress, being of a trusting nature. She was so ignorant of the ways of the world that it had never occurred to her that she had been grievously deceived, nor that her actions would have unwittingly angered her most beloved brother.

He and his sister left together for London the next day, where Darcy took steps to replace Mrs. Younge without delay. After consulting his cousin Fitzwilliam as joint guardian to Georgiana, Darcy was able to procure the services of Mrs. Annesley, a refined and pleasant woman who seemed to be well qualified to be a companion for his sister.

After a few days, her spirits began to revive, and she returned to her artistic pursuits, in drawing and her love of playing the piano-forte. The following week, Georgiana and Mrs. Annesley accompanied Darcy to Derbyshire, where his friend Charles Bingley joined them. He did not return to town until the early autumn when his sister's spirits were fully recovered. Bingley took a different route south, whilst Georgiana travelled with her brother.

4

The next week, Bingley arrived in town to stay with Darcy. He was full of a new enthusiasm for the counties north of London. On his journey, Bingley had been on a tour through Hertfordshire, and had been very taken by the country around the small town of Meryton.

Having found that a suitable property, Netherfield Park, was available, and after inspecting its situation and the principal rooms for half an hour, he had taken it on a short lease.

"So you see, Darcy," he said, "you must join me there. I shall take possession before Michaelmas. The sport for game in the park at Netherfield is promising, so we gentlemen at least will be well suited. I have hired servants who are to be in the house by the end of next week. I shall return to London once everything is settled there, and you and my sisters with Mr. Hurst must come down and join me."

"And I suppose," said his friend, "that you will try to convince me that I shall enjoy country ways and local assemblies . . ."

"But of course, my dear fellow!" said Bingley heartily, clapping his friend on the back. "And will Georgiana like to come with us?"

Darcy knew that his sister was very shy of being in any kind of company after her disappointment in Ramsgate. He had heard that Wickham had lately gone into the militia, although he knew not where. The manner in which her involvement with that gentleman had been dealt with hopefully meant that the affair never need be mentioned to anyone, least of all Bingley's sisters who delighted so in gossip.

Darcy had recently become aware that Georgiana did not find Miss Caroline Bingley very easy company, and did not welcome her staying with them at Pemberley. So he declined the pleasure of a visit to Hertfordshire on her behalf, using as the excuse that instruction with her music master would detain Georgiana in town with Mrs. Annesley.

Bingley was as good as his word, and some two weeks later was back in town to relate how his excursion into the country had gone.

He was able to report that his new neighbours had made him most welcome. Within a few days of his arrival in Hertfordshire, a number of gentlemen had waited on him.

One of the first of these had been a Mr. Bennet, a gentleman of limited fortune, who lived with his wife and five daughters in the largest house at Longbourn, a small place just outside Meryton. He had proved to be a man of sharp wits and literary conversation, aspects of character that were not Bingley's greatest strengths. However, the call had passed pleasantly enough.

Bingley had engaged to return his courtesy within a few days, having learned from other local acquaintances that the two eldest daughters, the Misses Jane and Elizabeth, were considered to be beauties and amongst the fairest young ladies in the County. On the next Friday, therefore, Bingley had ridden the mile over to Longbourn to return the visit.

He reported that it was a pleasant property, well situated, with an extensive shrubbery to one side but with modest grounds, and surrounded by its own farmland. Bingley had spent ten minutes with Mr. Bennet in his library, and was sorry to leave without having the opportunity of seeing any of the young ladies, although he had been glad to learn that the Misses Bennet enjoyed dancing.

A Sir William Lucas had also called, who was father to a large family and also lived in the neighbourhood of Nether-field. Bingley had been encouraged by Sir William to take a party to the next assembly in Meryton after his return to Hertfordshire.

"Is that not a capital plan?" said Bingley to his friend.

Darcy regarded him with a quizzical eye.

"I cannot recall how many times I have tried to impress upon you that my knowledge of the exercise is not matched by any enthusiasm for dancing with young ladies unknown to me."

"A ball is," he went on, "a vastly over-rated pastime, cal-culated to satisfy the desires of mothers who wish to expose me to their daughters with a view to marriage. The only re-sult is to require me to make conversation with the same tiresome young lady for half an hour at a time, without any chance of relief, whilst the whole of the room speculates on our future marriage and her good fortune!"

"Darcy," said his friend, "you are too sensitive. Of all the people I know, you are the most able to repel unwanted interest in a short sentence."

"But why invite such interest," Darcy replied, "if I do not wish to dance in the first place! I can not remember an occasion when I have obtained the pleasure you seem to find from taking the hand of a passably pretty woman in front of an assembled company."

Bingley protested. "It is high time, then, that you did encounter a young lady to interest you. And what better way than to meet the daughters of my new neighbours at a ball in the local assembly rooms?"

Since this appeared to be a subject on which they were unlikely to agree, Darcy did not pursue the point. Instead, he made sure that Georgiana was happily settled in town with Mrs. Annesley before he left with his friend for Hertfordshire, accompanied by Bingley's sisters and Mr. Hurst.

"My dear Mr. Darcy," said Caroline Bingley, "how will Louisa and I be able to support spending this whole evening at the ball at Meryton? I cannot abide country manners and noisy music! Can you not persuade my brother, even now, that we should stay here at home?"

"I fear not, Madam," said Darcy, who was leaning against the fireplace in the drawing room at Netherfield Park. "He is quite set on going, and on us accompanying him. I doubt very much whether Hertfordshire is as well provided with pretty young women as he has chosen to believe. But I regret that I have failed to persuade him to find any other better form of amusement acceptable for this evening."

At that moment, the object of their conversation entered the room, attired for the ball.

Miss Bingley pursued her attempt to divert their brother from his purpose. "Are you really determined," she said, "that we shall spend the evening with tradesmen's daughters and elderly dowagers?"

"I can never understand," replied her brother, "why you and Louisa must be so difficult to please, when we all have the prospect of such a pleasant evening in Meryton! Come, Darcy, all of you, a little social dancing will do you the world of good!"

And, within the hour, his chaise had delivered them to Meryton.

When they entered the assembly rooms, a group of musicians was busy playing a reel. All around him, it seemed to Darcy that very many ladies of all ages were regarding Bingley and his party with too much interest, whilst in the centre of all was an assortment of couples performing a dance with less than great ability. To Darcy, the evening did not seem to promise well.

The party from Netherfield was soon introduced to many of the company by Sir William Lucas, who took considerable pride in explaining to Darcy that he had been presented at court, and therefore was of some consequence in local society.

Within a few minutes, Darcy saw Bingley as usual quickly making the acquaintance of many of those assembled. His friend's easy manners and willingness to be pleased soon found favour with the company. He was lively and unreserved, was soon dancing every dance, expressed anger to learn that the ball closed so early, and talked of giving one himself at Netherfield.

Darcy observed all this as he walked about the room, averting his eyes from those he passed by, and hoping that

Bingley's sisters would return soon from dancing so that he had at least someone civilised to speak with.

He could not share his friend's pleasure in the evening. Sir William's attentions were intrusive, everywhere there seemed to be over-dressed matrons who looked up expectantly as he passed, eager to see whether he paused to ask one of their daughters to dance. The music was loud, the standard of dancing indifferent, and he saw no-one with whom any conversation could be a pleasure. He did observe that Bingley seemed much taken with the young lady who had been introduced as the elder Miss Bennet, a tall and graceful girl with pleasant manners, with whom he had danced twice.

During a break in the music, Bingley came over for a few minutes, to press his friend to join in.

"Come, Darcy," said he, "I must have you dance. I hate to see you standing about by yourself in this stupid manner. You had much better dance."

"I certainly shall not. You know how I detest it, unless I am particularly acquainted with my partner. At such an assembly as this, it would be insupportable. Your sisters are engaged, and there is not another woman in the room whom it would not be a punishment to me to stand up with."

"I would not be so fastidious as you are," cried Bingley, "for a kingdom! Upon my honour, I never met with so many pleasant girls in my life, as I have this evening; and there are several of them you can see uncommonly pretty."

"On the contrary, you are dancing with the only handsome girl in the room," said Darcy, looking at the eldest Miss Bennet.

"Oh! she is the most beautiful creature I ever beheld! But there is one of her sisters, Miss Elizabeth, sitting down just behind you, who is very pretty, and I dare say, very agreeable. Do let me ask my partner to introduce you."

"Which do you mean?" Darcy said. He turned round, and he looked for a moment at the young woman sitting close by till, catching her eye, he withdrew his own. She was talking to a tall serious young lady whom Sir William Lucas had introduced earlier as his eldest daughter.

"She is tolerable; but not handsome enough to tempt me," Darcy said.

"In any case, I am in no humour at present to give conse-quence to young ladies who are slighted by other men. You had better return to your partner and enjoy her smiles, for you are wasting your time with me."

Bingley protested but, having no success in his quest, he followed his friend's advice.

Darcy was left to reflect that with family, fortune and everything in his favour, he was entitled to do as he pleased. There was certainly no reason why he should dance with someone who, because of the scarcity of gentlemen, had been obliged to sit out two dances. Besides that, the conversation that he had overheard between her mother and younger sis-ters showed them to be vulgar, loud and ill-educated.

By the end of the evening, Darcy had danced once with Mrs. Hurst and once with Miss Bingley. He had rebuffed the efforts of Sir William Lucas to introduce him to any other ladies. He could recall nothing of enjoyment, no con-versation worth remembering. Indeed, his greatest pleasure was when the evening came to an end.

5

Bingley's company was welcome to Darcy precisely because they were so different in character and temperament. In understanding Darcy was the superior; Bingley was able, but his friend was clever. He was at the same time haughty, reserved, and fastidious, and his manners, though well bred, were not inviting. In that respect his friend had greatly the advantage. Bingley was sure of being liked wherever he appeared, whereas Darcy was continually giving offence.

A thoughtful observer might consider that Darcy's reluctance to mix in company might be due to the shyness inherited from his father as well as the position in the world on which some of his mother's family relied, regarding most people as not being worthy of notice. However, these were not considerations of which he was aware.

Darcy never spoke much away from familiar surroundings. Although he was one of the most attentive and best of brothers, only with his immediate family and close friends did he relax and, when he chose, could be very agreeable. Since he had yet to meet any lady whose approbation he wished to seek, Darcy in no way sought to hide his own distaste for company, and his resentment of the need to be sociable. Bingley's elder sister, Caroline, he acknowledged to have a sharp wit, and she was not always unwelcome when she accompanied her brother, but Darcy had never considered her as a possible wife for himself. She might be handsome in the current fashion, but her ignorance of books and country pursuits, and his own lack of interest in her person, ruled her out from being eligible.

The manner in which the Netherfield party spoke of the Meryton assembly thereafter was characteristic of both Bingley and his friend Darcy.

As far as the assembly at Meryton was concerned, Bingley had never met with pleasanter people or prettier girls in his life; everybody had been most kind and attentive to him, there had been no formality, no stiffness, and he had soon felt acquainted with all the room. As to the eldest Miss Bennet, he could not conceive an angel more beautiful. Darcy, on the contrary, had seen a collection of people in whom there was little beauty and no fashion, for none of whom he had felt the smallest interest, and from none received either attention or pleasure.

He commented that Bingley had danced with one of the few young women in the room, Miss Charlotte Lucas, who despite her father's apparent inability to make any serious conversation, had much that was sensible to say. Miss Bennet, Darcy acknowledged to be pretty, but she smiled too much, and as for the parents and younger sisters . . .

Mrs. Hurst and her sister allowed that Miss Jane Bennet

smiled rather often. However, having observed their brother's interest, they decided that they should pronounce her to be a sweet girl, and one whom they should not object to know more of. Darcy and his sisters' approbation was sufficient to encourage Bingley's continuing interest in the delightful Miss Bennet.

The Bennet ladies waited on those at Netherfield, and the visit was in due course returned. Caroline Bingley related to Darcy with relish the limited extent of the park at Longbourn, the worn and unfashionable furnishings in the house, and the vulgar and noisy behaviour of Mrs. Bennet and the youngest daughters. It was not, she said firmly, the type of company with which she usually associated, although she said again that the eldest Miss Bennet was a sweet, charming girl. She was not so complimentary about the second daughter, Miss Elizabeth, or her father, Mr. Bennet, both of whom she found too sharp, and too able to match her own wit.

In the fortnight after the Meryton assembly, Bingley and the eldest Miss Bennet met from time to time, although always in large mixed parties. Having danced four dances with her at Meryton; he saw her one morning at Netherfield, and dined in company with her on four occasions.

For Darcy, an unexpected consequence of Bingley's developing interest in that lady was that he found himself often in the company of her sister. Without first being aware of it, and against his will, Darcy found himself becoming conscious of the presence of Miss Elizabeth Bennet whenever they were together, and of his being disappointed when she was not present.

Having rejected his friend's opinion of her at Meryton, he had begun by assuming that she was, like her mother and her younger sisters Mary, Catherine and Lydia, well below his consideration. But no sooner had he made this very clear to himself and to his friends, than he began to find more than a passing pleasure in her lively expression, the quickness of mind displayed in her conversation, and the quality of her dark eyes. He had to concede that her figure was more than light and pleasing and he was caught by the easy playfulness of her manners.

As ever, he was not confident of his skills in discourse, but as a step towards speaking with her himself, Darcy began often to attend to her conversation with others.

A large party was assembled at Sir William Lucas's, and Darcy had been in a group with his host's eldest daughter, Charlotte, whom he had observed was often in company with her close friend, Miss Elizabeth.

Those attending the party included Colonel Forster, who commanded a regiment newly stationed at Meryton, and Darcy overheard Miss Elizabeth Bennet conversing with Miss Lucas.

"What does Mr. Darcy mean," said she, "by listening to my conversation with Colonel Forster?"

"That is a question which Mr. Darcy only can answer," Miss Lucas replied, looking in his direction.

He quickly turned away, in order that his interest should not be discovered, but not so far that he could not hear Miss Elizabeth Bennet's reply.

"But if he does it any more, I shall certainly let him know that I see what he is about. He has a very satirical eye, and if I do not begin by being impertinent myself, I shall soon grow afraid of him."

Darcy approached them more closely soon afterwards,

though without any intention of speaking. However, Miss Elizabeth Bennet turned to him and said, "Did not you think, Mr. Darcy, that I expressed myself uncommonly well just now, when I was teasing Colonel Forster to give us a ball at Meryton?"

Darcy found her liveliness very appealing and as quickly replied.

"With great energy; but it is a subject which always makes a lady energetic."

"You are severe on us."

Miss Lucas took pity on him.

"It will be her turn soon to be teased. I am going to open the instrument, Eliza, and you know what follows."

"You are a very strange creature by way of a friend, always wanting me to play and sing before anybody and everybody! If my vanity had taken a musical turn, you would have been invaluable, but as it is," and she looked at Darcy directly as she spoke, "I would really rather not sit down before those who must be in the habit of hearing the very best performers."

Unlike his usual response to flattery, Darcy found himself pleased that she had at least acknowledged him. He was not unwilling to hear her play, and on Miss Lucas's persevering, was pleased to hear Miss Bennet say, "Very well; if it must be so, it must."

She glanced at Darcy as she added, "There is a fine old saying, which every body here is of course familiar with 'Keep your breath to cool your porridge,' and I shall keep mine to swell my song."

Her performance was pleasing to Darcy's ear and he found that he had no wish for the recital to end.

But, after a few songs, she was eagerly succeeded at the instrument by her younger sister, Mary, who had neither genius nor taste, and had a pedantic air and conceited manner. Darcy decided, after hearing a few bars of the tune, that he had listened to Miss Elizabeth Bennet with much more pleasure, though she might not have played half so well.

At last Miss Mary Bennet was persuaded to play Scotch and Irish airs, at the request of her younger sisters who, with some of the Lucases and two or three officers joined eagerly in dancing at one end of the room. Since, as usual, Darcy disdained to dance, he stood observing, in silent indignation at such a mode of passing the evening, to the exclusion of all conversation.

He was thus occupied, so as to be unaware that his host had approached him, till Sir William began.

"What a charming amusement for young people this is, Mr. Darcy! There is nothing like dancing after all. I consider it as one of the first refinements of polished societies."

"Certainly, Sir; and it has the advantage also of being in vogue amongst the less polished societies of the world. Every savage can dance."

Although Darcy had intended this comment to silence him, Sir William only smiled.

"Your friend performs delightfully," he continued after a pause, on seeing Bingley join the group, "and I doubt not that you are an adept in the science yourself, Mr. Darcy."

"You saw me dance at Meryton, I believe, Sir."

"Yes, indeed, and received no inconsiderable pleasure from the sight. Do you often dance at St. James's?"

"Never, Sir," said Darcy, again hoping that Sir William would desist.

"Do you not think it would be a proper compliment to the place?"

"It is a compliment which I never pay to any place if I can avoid it."

"You have a house in town, I conclude?"

Darcy bowed. He hoped by saying nothing to end the conversation, but Sir William was not so easily disconcerted.

"I had once some thoughts of fixing in town myself, for I am fond of superior society; but I did not feel quite certain that the air of London would agree with Lady Lucas."

He paused, but Darcy was not disposed to make any answer.

At that moment, on Miss Elizabeth Bennet moving towards them, his host called out to her,

"My dear Miss Eliza, why are not you dancing? Mr. Darcy, you must allow me to present this young lady to you as a very desirable partner. You cannot refuse to dance, I am sure, when so much beauty is before you."

Taking Miss Bennet's hand, Sir William would have given it to him, and he was not unwilling to receive it.

She however drew back and said, "Indeed, Sir, I have not the least intention of dancing. I entreat you not to suppose that I moved this way in order to beg for a partner."

At this, Darcy found himself to be genuine in requesting to be allowed the honour of her hand for the next dance. To his surprise, for he was certainly not accustomed to such an answer, she persisted in her refusal.

Sir William made a further attempt at persuasion.

"You excel so much in the dance, Miss Eliza, that it is cruel to deny me the happiness of seeing you; and though this gentleman dislikes the amusement in general, he can have no objection, I am sure, to oblige us for one half hour."

"Mr. Darcy is all politeness," said Miss Elizabeth Bennet, smiling slightly, so that he thought that this time she might agree.

"He is indeed but, considering the inducement, my dear Miss Eliza, we cannot wonder at his complaisance; for who would object to such a partner?"

Miss Bennet looked as though to speak, but then turned away.

To Darcy, her response was a refreshing contrast to his usual experience, and did not damage his opinion of her. His eyes followed as she crossed the room to talk to the eldest Miss Lucas, and he was thinking of her with pleasure when he was accosted by Miss Bingley.

"I can guess the subject of your reverie."

"I should imagine not."

"You are considering how insupportable it would be to pass many evenings in this manner in such society; and indeed I am quite of your opinion. I was never more annoyed!"

Darcy, very used to her manner of speaking, did not consider that this merited a reply.

"The insipidity and yet the noise; the nothingness and yet the self-importance of all these people! What would I give to hear your strictures on them!"

Darcy was at first inclined to maintain his silence, but then decided that what she had ventured deserved contradiction.

"Your conjecture is totally wrong, I assure you. My mind was more agreeably engaged. I have been meditating on the very great pleasure which a pair of fine eyes in the face of a pretty woman can bestow."

Hoping that he was alluding to herself, Miss Bingley desired he would tell her what lady had the credit of inspiring such reflections.

He replied without any hesitation, "Miss Elizabeth Bennet."

"Miss Elizabeth Bennet!" repeated Miss Bingley, by turns angry and mortified. "I am all astonishment. How long has she been such a favourite? and pray, when am I to wish you joy?"

"That is exactly the question which I expected you to ask," Darcy replied calmly. "A lady's imagination is very rapid; it jumps from admiration to love, from love to matrimony, in a moment. I knew you would be wishing me joy."

"Nay, if you are so serious about it, I shall consider the matter as absolutely settled. You will have a charming mother-in-law, indeed, and of course she will be always at Pemberley with you."

He listened to her without comment, whilst reflecting that his sister's opinion of Miss Bingley was perhaps very fair.

Despite his silence, she chose to entertain herself by continuing in this vein for some time, but Darcy took no notice, being as usual unconcerned with any opinion contrary to his own.

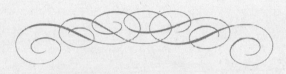

Part Two

He never speaks much unless amongst his intimate acquaintance . . .
but . . . Mr. Darcy has no defect. He owns it himself without any disguise.

6

On the following day, since Bingley and Darcy were to dine with the officers of the regiment, Caroline Bingley sent a note by a servant to Longbourn, to invite Miss Jane Bennet to join the two sisters for dinner that evening.

When the gentlemen returned, it was raining, and they were greeted with the news that Miss Bennet had indeed travelled to Netherfield, but on horseback. The consequence of her not travelling in her father's carriage meant that she was to remain overnight. The next morning it soon became clear that her damp journey had resulted in Miss Bennet catching a chill, with a sore throat.

Bingley and his sisters would not hear of her returning home until she was better, so a note was sent to tell Miss Elizabeth Bennet that Mr. Jones the apothecary had been called, although there was no cause for alarm. When Darcy looked out of the window a few hours later, it was with some considerable surprise that he saw that same lady trudging across the lawns in front of Netherfield House.

When she was shown into the breakfast parlour, where Bingley and the others were all seated, it was clear from the state of her skirts that she must have walked all the 3 miles from Longbourn. When this was questioned by Miss Bingley, Miss Elizabeth Bennet explained that she was no horsewoman and enjoyed walking. She asked anxiously to be taken immediately to see her sister.

As she left the room, Darcy could not help but note that her face was glowing with the warmth of the exercise, although he doubted whether she should have come so far alone. Two of those present had less charitable matters on their mind. That she should have walked three miles so early in the day, in such dirty weather, and by herself, was almost incredible to Mrs. Hurst and Miss Bingley, and they commented upon it at length. Darcy did not support their criticisms, and Mr. Hurst said nothing at all, since he was thinking only of his breakfast.

It soon became clear that Miss Bennet had not slept well, being very feverish and not well enough to leave her room. When breakfast was over, the apothecary came and, having examined his patient, said that she had caught a violent cold, and advised her to return to bed, promising to provide some draughts. The advice was followed readily, since her feverish symptoms had apparently increased, together with a headache.

That morning, Darcy and Bingley went out to shoot with Mr. Hurst and, when they returned, found that Miss Bingley had offered Miss Elizabeth Bennet the carriage for her return journey. However, her elder sister had been so concerned at her leaving that the offer had to be converted into an invitation for her to remain at Netherfield for the present.

Darcy was not unhappy that this offer was accepted, and in due course to see Miss Elizabeth Bennet summoned to dinner. To the enquiries that were made, she could not respond with a very favourable answer and, after dinner, she returned directly to her sister's room.

Miss Bingley began abusing her as soon as she was gone. Her manners were pronounced to be very bad indeed, a mixture of pride and impertinence; she had no conversation, no style, no taste, no beauty. Mrs. Hurst thought the same, and added,

"She has nothing, in short, to recommend her, but being an excellent walker. I shall never forget her appearance this morning. She really looked almost wild."

"She did indeed, Louisa. I could hardly keep my countenance. Very nonsensical to come at all! Why must she be scampering about the country, because her sister had a cold? Her hair so untidy, so blowsy!"

"Yes, and her petticoat; I hope you saw her petticoat, six inches deep in mud, I am absolutely certain; and the gown which had been let down to hide it, not doing its office."

"Your picture may be very exact, Louisa," said Bingley; who had been listening to this conversation with little enthusiasm, "but this was all lost upon me. I thought Miss Elizabeth Bennet looked remarkably well when she came into the room this morning. Her dirty petticoat quite escaped my notice."

"You observed it, Mr. Darcy, I am sure," said Miss Bingley, "and I am inclined to think that you would not wish to see your sister make such an exhibition."

"Certainly not."

"To walk three miles, or four miles, or five miles, or whatever it is, above her ankles in dirt, and alone, quite alone! What could she mean by it? It seems to me to show an abominable sort of conceited independence, a most country town indifference to decorum."

"It shows an affection for her sister that is very pleasing," said Bingley.

"I am afraid, Mr. Darcy," observed Miss Bingley, in a half whisper, "that this adventure has rather affected your admiration of her fine eyes."

He was not inclined to indulge her, and replied, "Not at all, they were brightened by the exercise."

A short pause followed this. Then Mrs. Hurst began again.

"I have an excessive regard for Jane Bennet, she is really a very sweet girl, and I wish with all my heart she were well settled. But with such a father and mother, and such low connections, I am afraid there is no chance of it."

"I think I have heard you say, that their uncle is an attorney in Meryton."

"Yes, and they have another, who lives somewhere near Cheapside."

"That is capital," added her sister, and they both laughed heartily.

"If they had uncles enough to fill all Cheapside," said Bingley, mindful that their own father had made his fortune from trade, "it would not make them one jot less agreeable."

"But it must very materially lessen their chance of marrying men of any consideration in the world," replied Darcy, who had found by experience that his friend did not always by any means share his concern for the niceties of social standing and consequence.

Bingley did not reply, but his sisters gave this view their hearty assent, and they went on to indulge their mirth for some time at the expense of Miss Bennet's vulgar relations.

Miss Elizabeth Bennet would not quit her sister till late in the evening. When she entered the drawing-room, the whole party was at loo, and she was immediately invited to join them. Making her sister the excuse, she said that she would amuse herself with a book for the short time she could stay below. Mr. Hurst looked at her with astonishment.

"Do you prefer reading to cards?" said he; "that is rather singular."

Miss Bingley could not resist making a point from this.

"Miss Eliza Bennet despises cards. She is a great reader and has no pleasure in anything else."

The object of her scorn looked surprised at this attack, but replied quietly, "I deserve neither such praise nor such censure. I am not a great reader, and I have pleasure in many things."

This seemed a satisfactory answer to Darcy, and his friend's comments were to the same effect.

"In nursing your sister, I am sure you will have pleasure, and I hope it will soon be increased by seeing her quite well."

Miss Bennet thanked him, and then walked towards a table where a few books were lying. Bingley immediately offered to fetch her others from his library, but she assured him that she could suit herself perfectly with those in the room.

"I am astonished," said Miss Bingley, "that my father

should have left so small a collection of books. What a delightful library you have at Pemberley, Mr. Darcy!"

"It ought to be good," he replied, "it has been the work of many generations."

"And then you have added so much to it yourself, you are always buying books."

He was not sure that this was a commendation, but replied, "I cannot comprehend the neglect of a family library in such days as these."

"Neglect! I am sure you neglect nothing that can add to the beauties of that noble place. Charles, when you build your house, I wish it may be half as delightful as Pemberley."

"I wish it may," her brother replied.

"But I would really advise you to make your purchase in that neighbourhood, and take Pemberley for a kind of model. There is not a finer county in England than Derbyshire."

"With all my heart; I will buy Pemberley itself if Darcy will sell it."

"I am talking of possibilities, Charles."

"Upon my word, Caroline, I should think it more possible to get Pemberley by purchase than by imitation."

Darcy then saw that Miss Elizabeth Bennet laid her book aside. She moved to stand near the card-table between Mr. Bingley and his eldest sister to observe the game.

"Is Miss Darcy much grown since the spring?" said Miss Bingley; "will she be as tall as I am?"

Darcy looked at her for a moment, and then turned to her guest as he said, "I think she will. She is now about Miss Elizabeth Bennet's height, or rather taller."

"How I long to see her again! I never met with anybody who delighted me so much. Such a countenance, such manners! and so extremely accomplished for her age! Her performance on the piano-forte is exquisite."

"It is amazing to me," said Bingley, "how young ladies can have patience to be so very accomplished, as they all are."

"All young ladies accomplished! My dear Charles, what do you mean?" said his sister.

"Yes, all of them, I think. They all paint tables, cover screens and net purses.

I scarcely know any one who cannot do all this, and I am sure I never heard a young lady spoken of for the first time, without being informed that she was very accomplished."

"Your list of the common extent of accomplishments," said Darcy, "has too much truth. The word is applied to many a woman who deserves it no otherwise than by netting a purse, or covering a screen. But I am very far from agreeing with you in your estimation of ladies in general. I cannot boast of knowing more than half a dozen, in the whole range of my acquaintance, that are really accomplished."

"Nor I, I am sure," said Miss Bingley, quick to agree with him.

"Then," observed Miss Elizabeth Bennet to Darcy, "you must comprehend a great deal in your idea of an accomplished woman." She half smiled at him as she spoke, and Darcy was tempted to do so in kind, as he said, "Yes; I do comprehend a great deal in it."

"Oh! certainly," cried Miss Bingley to Darcy, not wishing to be overlooked, "no one can be really esteemed accomplished, who does not greatly surpass what is usually met with."

Since he said nothing, she went on, "A woman must have a thorough knowledge of music, singing, drawing, dancing, and the modern languages, to deserve the word; and besides all this, she must possess a certain something in her air and manner of walking, the tone of her voice, her address and expressions, or the word will be but half deserved."

"All this she must possess," added Darcy, addressing Miss Bennet, "and to all this she must yet add something more substantial, in the improvement of her mind by extensive reading."

"I am no longer surprised at your knowing only six accomplished women. I rather wonder now at your knowing any," said Miss Elizabeth Bennet.

Darcy was not sure whether she doubted the idea, or his own opinion.

"Are you so severe upon your own sex, as to doubt the possibility of all this?"

"I never saw such a woman," Miss Bennet replied, "I never saw such capacity, and taste, and application, and elegance, as you describe, united."

Both Mrs. Hurst and Miss Bingley protested at this, saying that they knew many women who answered this description. But Mr. Hurst then called them to order, with bitter complaints of their inattention.

It was with regret that Darcy saw Miss Bennet soon afterwards leave the room.

"Eliza Bennet," said Miss Bingley, when the door was closed on her, "is one of those young ladies who seek to recommend themselves to the other sex, by undervaluing their own; and with many men, I dare say, it succeeds."

She looked to the others for a reaction, but in vain, so she went on, "But, in my opinion, it is a paltry device, a very mean art."

"Undoubtedly," replied Darcy, to whom this remark was chiefly addressed, "there is meanness in all the arts which ladies sometimes condescend to employ for captivation. Whatever bears affinity to cunning is despicable."

As he had intended, Miss Bingley was not so entirely satisfied with his reply as to continue the subject.

Miss Elizabeth Bennet joined them again only to say that her sister was worse, and that she could not leave her. Bingley urged Mr. Jones's being sent for immediately; while his sisters recommended that an express be sent for one of the most eminent physicians from town. This, she did not agree to, but it was settled that Mr. Jones should be sent for early in the morning, if Miss Bennet were not decidedly better.

7

Miss Elizabeth Bennet in the morning was able to send a better answer to the enquiries that she very early received from Bingley, but requested to have a note sent to Longbourn, desiring her mother to visit her sister, and form her own judgement of her situation.

Although this was not a prospect that Darcy, or Bingley's sisters, viewed with any enthusiasm, the note was immediately dispatched, and its contents as quickly complied with, and Mrs. Bennet, accompanied by her youngest daughters, Catherine and Lydia, reached Netherfield soon after breakfast.

On being satisfied on seeing her that her eldest daughter's illness was not alarming, she would not listen to her being moved home; neither did the apothecary, who arrived about the same time, think it at all advisable. After sitting a little while with her daughter, on Miss Bingley's appearance and invitation, the mother and three younger daughters all attended their hostess into the breakfast parlour, where they found Darcy with his friend.

Bingley met them with hopes that Mrs. Bennet had not found Miss Jane worse than she expected.

"Indeed, Sir, she is a great deal too ill to be moved. Mr. Jones says we must not think of moving her. We must trespass a little longer on your kindness."

"Removed!" cried Bingley. "It must not be thought of. My sister, I am sure, will not hear of her removal."

"You may depend upon it, Madam," said Miss Bingley, with cold civility, "that Miss Bennet shall receive every possible attention while she remains with us."

Mrs. Bennet was profuse in her acknowledgements. "I am sure," she added, "if it was not for such good friends I do not know what would become of her, for she is very ill indeed, and suffers a vast deal, though with the greatest patience in the world, which is always the way with her, for she has, without exception, the sweetest temper I ever met with. I often tell my other girls they are nothing to her. You have a sweet room here, Mr. Bingley, and a charming prospect over that gravel walk. I do not know a place in the country that is equal to Netherfield. You will not think of quitting it in a hurry I hope, though you have but a short lease."

"Whatever I do is done in a hurry," replied he; "and therefore if I should resolve to quit Netherfield, I should probably be off in five minutes. At present, however, I consider myself as quite fixed here."

"That is exactly what I should have supposed of you," said Miss Elizabeth Bennet.

Darcy, who had been looking out of the window hoping that Mrs. Bennet's stay would be curtailed, turned to look with more interest at what was being said on hearing her daughter's voice.

"You begin to comprehend me, do you?" replied Bingley.

"Oh! yes—I understand you perfectly."

"I wish I might take this for a compliment; but to be so easily seen through I am afraid is pitiful."

"That is as it happens," said Miss Elizabeth, "it does not necessarily follow that a deep, intricate character is more or less estimable than such a one as yours."

"Lizzy," cried her mother, "remember where you are, and do not run on in the wild manner that you are suffered to do at home."

"I did not know before," continued Bingley immediately to her daughter, "that you were a studier of character. It must be an amusing study."

"Yes; but intricate characters are the most amusing. They have at least that advantage."

"The country," said Darcy, in a bid to gain her attention, "can in general supply but few subjects for such a study. In a country neighbourhood you move in a very confined and unvarying society."

Miss Elizabeth did not dissent to that, and added, "But people themselves alter so much, that there is something new to be observed in them for ever."

To Darcy's regret, they were then interrupted.

"Yes, indeed," cried Mrs. Bennet, looking most offended, "I assure you there is quite as much of that going on in the country as in town."

Darcy, after looking at her for a moment, turned silently away. Mrs. Bennet, who fancied she had triumphed over him, persisted.

"I cannot see that London has any great advantage over the country for my part, exeept the shops and public places. The country is a vast deal pleasanter, is not it, Mr. Bingley?"

"When I am in the country," he replied, "I never wish to leave it; and when I am in town it is pretty much the same. They have each their advantages, and I can be equally happy in either."

"Aye—that is because you have the right disposition. But that gentleman," said Mrs. Bennet, looking straight at Darcy, "seemed to think the country was nothing at all."

"Indeed, Mama, you are mistaken," said Miss Elizabeth Bennet, blushing for her mother. "You quite mistook Mr. Darcy. He only meant that there were not such a variety of people to be met with in the country as in town, which you must acknowledge to be true."

"Certainly, my dear, nobody said there were; but as to not meeting with many people in this neighbourhood, I believe there are few neighbourhoods larger. I know we dine with four and twenty families."

Darcy observed that Miss Elizabeth Bennet, for the sake of saying something that might turn her mother's thoughts, now asked Mrs. Bennet if her friend Charlotte Lucas had been at Longbourn since her coming away.

"Yes, she called yesterday with her father. What an agreeable man Sir William is, Mr. Bingley—is not he? so much the man of fashion! So genteel and so easy! He has always something to say to every body. That is my idea of good breeding; and those persons who fancy themselves very important and," looking at Darcy as she spoke, "never open their mouths, quite mistake the matter."

"Did Charlotte dine with you?" asked Miss Elizabeth.

"No, she would go home. I fancy she was wanted about the mince pies. For my part, Mr. Bingley, I always keep servants that can do their own work; my daughters are brought up differently. But every body is to judge for themselves, and the Lucases are a very good sort of girls, I assure you. It is a pity they are not handsome! Not that I think Charlotte so very plain—but then she is our particular friend."

"She seems a very pleasant young woman," said Bingley.

"Oh! dear, yes; but you must own she is very plain. Lady Lucas herself has often said so, and envied me Jane's beauty. I do not like to boast of my own child, but to be sure, one does not often see anybody better looking. It is what every body says. I do not trust my own partiality. When she was only fifteen, there was a gentleman at my brother Gardiner's in town, so much in love with her, that my sister-in-law was sure he would make her an offer before we came away. But however he did not. Perhaps he thought her too young. However, he wrote some verses on her, and very pretty they were."

"And so ended his affection," said Miss Elizabeth scornfully. "There has been many a one, I fancy, overcome in the same way. I wonder who first discovered the efficacy of poetry in driving away love!"

Darcy was surprised at this answer and decided to venture a reply.

"I have been used to consider poetry as the food of love," said he.

"Of a fine, stout, healthy love it may. Every thing nourishes what is strong already." Miss Elizabeth paused, but then in her lively way added, "But if it be only a slight, thin sort of inclination, I am convinced that one good sonnet will starve it entirely away."

Darcy smiled at this; but said nothing. A general pause ensued, until Mrs. Bennet repeated her thanks to Bingley for his kindness to her eldest daughter, with an apology for troubling him also with her sister, and soon afterwards ordered her carriage.

At this, her youngest daughter, Lydia, a stout, well-grown girl of fifteen, taxed Bingley with having promised on his first coming into the country to give a ball at Netherfield, adding that it would be the most shameful thing in the world if he did not keep it.

His answer to this sudden attack was more civil than Darcy thought that it deserved, contrasting her very forward style of address with that of his sister. However, Bingley as ever refused to be affronted.

"I am perfectly ready, I assure you, to keep my engagement; and when your sister is recovered, you shall if you please name the very day of the ball. But you would not wish to be dancing while she is ill."

"Oh! yes it would be much better to wait till Jane was well, and by that time most likely Captain Carter would be at Meryton again. And when you have given your ball," she added, "I shall insist on their giving one also. I shall tell Colonel Forster it will be quite a shame if he does not."

Mrs. Bennet and her daughters then departed, and Miss Elizabeth Bennet returned instantly to her sister, leaving her own and her relations' behaviour to the remarks of the two ladies.

Darcy, however, could not be prevailed on to join in their censure of her, in spite of all Miss Bingley's witticisms on fine eyes.

8

The next day, the invalid kept to her bed but continued, though slowly, to mend; and in the evening Miss Elizabeth Bennet joined the party in the drawing-room.

Darcy was writing, and thus continued, although he was very aware of her entering the room, and taking up some needlework.

Mr. Hurst and Bingley were at piquet, and Mrs. Hurst was observing their game. Miss Bingley, seated nearer to Darcy, had been watching the progress of his letter, and repeatedly disturbed him by calling his attention to her messages to his sister.

The perpetual commendations of the lady either on his handwriting, or on the evenness of his lines, or on the length of his letter, formed a conversation that increasingly began to irritate Darcy.

"How delighted Miss Darcy will be to receive such a letter!"

He made no answer.

"You write uncommonly fast."

He wrote two more lines before replying, "You are mistaken. I write rather slowly."

"How many letters you must have occasion to write in the course of the year! Letters of business too! How odious I should think them!"

Again he continued writing for some time before saying, "It is fortunate, then, that they fall to my lot instead of to yours."

He hoped that she would then desist, but it was not to be.

"Pray tell your sister that I long to see her."

He looked back at what he had already penned, and then said sharply, "I have already told her so once, by your desire."

A few welcome minutes of silence then ensued. He even had some hopes that he might be able to finish the letter uninterrupted, and he paused, considering the last few sentences he had written. But Caroline Bingley's voice was then again heard addressing him.

"I am afraid you do not like your pen. Let me mend it for you."

When he did not reply, she tried again.

"I mend pens remarkably well."

"Thank you—but I always mend my own."

"How can you contrive to write so even?"

He was silent.

"Tell your sister I am delighted to hear of her improvement on the harp, and pray let her know that I am quite in raptures with her beautiful little design for a table, and I think it infinitely superior to Miss Grantley's."

By this time, Darcy's temper was rising, and it was with difficulty that he remained civil, especially as he would much rather be conversing with Miss Elizabeth Bennet.

"Will you give me leave to defer your raptures till I write again? At present I have not room to do them justice."

"Oh! it is of no consequence. I shall see her in January. But do you always write such charming long letters to her, Mr. Darcy?"

He began to wonder if there were any means by which Miss Bingley could be silenced.

"They are generally long; but whether always charming, it is not for me to determine."

"It is a rule with me, that a person who can write a long letter, with ease, cannot write ill," she said.

"That will not do for a compliment to Darcy, Caroline," cried her brother, "because he does not write with ease. He studies too much for words of four syllables. Do not you, Darcy?"

Darcy was relieved at another person joining in the conversation, and said, more cheerfully, "My style of writing is very different from yours."

"Oh!" cried Miss Bingley, "Charles writes in the most careless way imaginable. He leaves out half his words, and blots the rest."

"My ideas flow so rapidly that I have not time to express them by which means my letters sometimes convey no ideas at all to my correspondents," said her brother.

At this point, an interruption very welcome to Darcy was made, as Miss Elizabeth Bennet said, "Your humility, Mr. Bingley, must disarm reproof."

"Nothing is more deceitful," said Darcy, with the intention of provoking her, rather than his friend, to say more, "than the appearance of humility. It is often only carelessness of opinion, and sometimes an indirect boast."

He was unsuccessful, for it was Bingley who said, "And which of the two do you call my little recent piece of modesty?"

With Miss Bennet's attention still engaged, Darcy was ready for a debate.

"The indirect boast; for you are really proud of your defects in writing, because you consider them as proceeding from a rapidity of thought and carelessness of execution, which if not estimable, you think at least highly interesting. The power of doing anything with quickness is always much prized by the possessor, and often without any attention to the imperfection of the performance. When you told Mrs. Bennet this morning that if you ever resolved on quitting Netherfield you should be gone in five minutes, you meant it to be a sort of panegyric, of compliment to yourself and yet what is there so very laudable in a precipitance which must leave very necessary business undone, and can be of no real advantage to yourself or any one else?"

After this, Darcy thought it certain that Miss Bennet's lively mind would join her into the conversation. But Bingley was too quick.

"Nay," he cried, "this is too much, to remember at night all the foolish things that were said in the morning. And yet, upon my honour, I believed what I said of myself to be true, and I believe it at this moment. At least, therefore, I did not assume the character of needless precipitance merely to show off before the ladies."

"I dare say you believed it; but I am by no means con-

vinced that you would be gone with such celerity," said
Darcy. "Your conduct would be quite as dependent on
chance as that of any man I know; and if, as you were mounting your horse, a friend were to say, 'Bingley, you had better
stay till next week,' you would probably do it, you would
probably not go and, at another word, might stay a month."

At last, this provoked Miss Elizabeth Bennet to join in
the conversation.

"You have only proved by this, that Mr. Bingley did not
do justice to his own disposition. You have shown him off
now much more than he did himself."

"I am exceedingly gratified," said Bingley, "by your con-
verting what my friend says into a compliment on the sweetness of my temper. But I am afraid you are giving it a turn
which that gentleman did by no means intend; for he would
certainly think the better of me, if under such a circumstance
I were to give a flat denial, and ride off as fast as I could."

"Would Mr. Darcy then consider the rashness of your
original intention as atoned for by your obstinacy in adher-
ing to it?" Miss Bennet said to him.

"Upon my word I cannot exactly explain the matter,
Darcy must speak for himself."

"You expect me to account for opinions which you
choose to call mine, but which I have never acknowledged,"
said Darcy. "Allowing the case, however, to stand according
to your representation, you must remember, Miss Bennet,
that the friend who is supposed to desire his return to the
house, and the delay of his plan, has merely desired it, asked
it without offering one argument in favour of its propriety."

"To yield readily—easily—to the persuasion of a friend is
no merit with you." She looked at Darcy thoughtfully.

"To yield without conviction is no compliment to the understanding of either," he replied to her.

"You appear to me, Mr. Darcy, to allow nothing for the influence of friendship and affection. A regard for the requester would often make one readily yield to a request, without waiting for arguments to reason one into it. I am not particularly speaking of such a case as you have supposed about Mr. Bingley."

She paused as though to consider the matter further, and then went on, "We may as well wait, perhaps, till the circumstance occurs, before we discuss the discretion of his behaviour thereupon."

He was about to reply, but then she turned to him with renewed inspiration.

"But in general and ordinary cases between friend and friend, where one of them is desired by the other to change a resolution of no very great moment, should you think ill of that person for complying with the desire, without waiting to be argued into it?"

"Will it not be advisable, before we proceed on this subject," said Darcy, "to arrange with rather more precision the degree of importance which is to appertain to this request, as well as the degree of intimacy subsisting between the parties?"

"By all means," interrupted Bingley; "let us hear all the particulars, not forgetting their comparative height and size; for that will have more weight in the argument, Miss Bennet, than you may be aware of. I assure you that if Darcy were not such a great tall fellow, in comparison with myself, I should not pay him half so much deference."

Darcy was amused and was ready to respond with some humour. However, Bingley forestalled him.

"I declare, Miss Elizabeth, I do not know a more aweful object than Darcy, on particular occasions, and in particular places; at his own house especially, and of a Sunday evening when he has nothing to do."

Darcy knew himself to be looking affronted at this, and smiled rather wanly.

Miss Bingley intervened to join the conversation, in an expostulation with her brother for talking such nonsense.

"I see your design, Bingley," said his friend. "You dislike an argument, and want to silence this."

"Perhaps I do. Arguments are too much like disputes. If you and Miss Bennet will defer yours till I am out of the room, I shall be very thankful; and then you may say whatever you like of me."

"What you ask," said Miss Elizabeth Bennet, "is no sacrifice on my side; and Mr. Darcy had much better finish his letter."

Darcy took her advice, and did finish his letter.

With that over, he applied to Miss Bingley and Miss Elizabeth Bennet for the indulgence of some music.

Miss Bingley moved with alacrity to the piano-forte, and after a polite request that Miss Elizabeth Bennet would lead the way, which the other as politely and more earnestly resisted, she seated herself and sang with Mrs. Hurst.

Whilst they were thus employed, Darcy regarded Miss Elizabeth Bennet with a steady gaze.

Once or twice she looked up and caught his expression, and as quickly looked away again as she turned over some music books that lay on the instrument. As the music continued, he was taken with what for him was a novel and irrational thought. He almost wished, yes indeed he did wish, to take a turn around the floor with her.

As though aware of his thoughts, after finishing some Italian songs, Miss Bingley changed the style of her music, and began to play a Scottish air.

Emboldened by this happy coincidence, Darcy said, "Do not you feel a great inclination, Miss Bennet, to seize such an opportunity of dancing a reel?"

She made no answer. He repeated the question, with some surprise at her silence.

"Oh!" said she, "I heard you before; but I could not immediately determine what to say in reply."

She gave him again that lively smile as she went on, "You wanted me, I know, to say 'Yes,' that you might have the pleasure of despising my taste; but I always delight in overthrowing those kind of schemes, and cheating a person of their premeditated contempt. I have therefore made up my mind to tell you, that I do not want to dance a reel at all and now despise me if you dare."

He replied civilly, although he was disappointed out of proportion to the request.

"Indeed," said Darcy, "I do not dare."

Yet he did not resent the answer as he might have done, for there was a mixture of sweetness and archness in her manner that made it difficult for her to affront him. Had Darcy been able to consider the matter dispassionately, he would have realised that he had never been so bewitched by any woman as he was by her. But for the inferiority of her connections, he was of the opinion that he should be in some danger.

9

Miss Bingley was not unaware of Darcy's interest in her guest. She was not of a disposition to overlook such a slight, and frequently sought to provoke Darcy by talking of their supposed marriage, and planning his happiness in such an alliance.

"I hope," said she, as they were walking together in the shrubbery the next day, "you will give your mother-in-law a few hints, when this desirable event takes place, as to the advantage of holding her tongue; and if you can compass it, do cure the younger girls of running after the officers. And, if I may mention so delicate a subject, endeavour to check that little something, bordering on conceit and impertinence, which your lady possesses."

Darcy was not one to allow himself to be upset unless he particularly valued the opinion of the speaker. He took this attempt to challenge him calmly, as he did Miss Bingley's next comment that Mrs. Bennet was a woman of mean understanding and uncertain temper, who might prove less than a worthy addition to his acquaintance.

"Have you anything else to propose for my domestic felicity?" he said.

"Oh! yes. Do let the portraits of your uncle and aunt Philips be placed in the gallery at Pemberley. Put them next to your great uncle the judge. They are in the same profession, you know; only in different lines. As for your Elizabeth's picture, you must not attempt to have it taken, for what painter could do justice to those beautiful eyes?"

"It would not be easy, indeed, to catch their expression, but their colour and shape, and the eye-lashes, so remarkably fine, might be copied."

At that moment they were met from another walk, by Mrs. Hurst and Miss Elizabeth Bennet herself.

"I did not know that you intended to walk," said Miss Bingley, in some confusion, lest they had been overheard.

"You used us abominably ill," answered Mrs. Hurst, "in running away without telling us that you were coming out."

Then taking the disengaged arm of Mr. Darcy, she left Miss Elizabeth to walk by herself, as the path just admitted three.

Darcy resented this affront on her behalf and, not wishing to lose her company, said, "This walk is not wide enough for our party. We had better go into the avenue."

And he waited for Miss Bennet to join them.

But she answered, with a smile,

"No, no; stay where you are. You are charmingly grouped, and appear to uncommon advantage. The picturesque would be spoilt by admitting a fourth. Good bye."

Contrary to Darcy's preference, she then went off, and

he was left to wish that he had different company from Miss Bingley, whose wit was so repetitive and often seemed to be at his own expense.

Miss Jane Bennet was already recovered enough to leave her room for a couple of hours that evening after dinner. Her sister attended her, well guarded from cold, into the drawing-room.

When the gentlemen entered, Darcy addressed himself directly to Miss Bennet, with a polite congratulation; Mr. Hurst also made her a slight bow, and Bingley sat down by her.

Darcy, preferring the chance of conversation with Miss Elizabeth Bennet to playing with cards, had declined to join Mr. Hurst in his favourite pastime. Mr. Hurst had therefore nothing to do, but to stretch himself on one of the sofas and go to sleep.

Darcy took up a book, and so Miss Bingley did the same. Mrs. Hurst, principally occupied in playing with her bracelets and rings, joined now and then in her brother's conversation with Miss Bennet.

Miss Bingley gave as much attention to watching Mr. Darcy's progress through his book as to reading her own; and she was perpetually either making some inquiry, or looking at his page. He, however, had no intention of being persuaded into any conversation with her, and so limited himself to answering her questions, and then read on.

At length, she gave a great yawn and said, "How pleasant it is to spend an evening in this way! I declare after all there is no enjoyment like reading! How much sooner one tires of anything than of a book! When I have a house of my own, I shall be miserable if I have not an excellent library."

Darcy reflected to himself that she would not be an easy companion to any man, and no one made any reply.

She then yawned again, threw aside her book, and cast her eyes round the room in quest of some amusement. When her brother mentioned a ball to Miss Bennet, she turned suddenly towards him and said, "By the bye, Charles, are you really serious in meditating a dance at Netherfield? I would advise you, before you determine on it, to consult the wishes of the present party."

Looking at his friend, she said, "I am much mistaken if there are not some among us to whom a ball would be rather a punishment than a pleasure."

"If you mean Darcy," cried her brother, "he may go to bed, if he chooses, before it begins, but as for the ball, it is quite a settled thing; and as soon as Nicholls has made white soup enough I shall send round my cards."

"I should like balls infinitely better," she replied, "if they carried on in a different manner; but there is something insufferably tedious in the usual process of such a meeting. It would surely be much more rational if conversation instead of dancing made the order of the day."

If she had hoped to persuade Darcy to join in the conversation, she was not successful. Instead, her brother persisted.

"Much more rational, my dear Caroline, I dare say, but it would not be near so much like a ball."

Miss Bingley made no answer; and soon afterwards got up and walked about the room. Darcy continued his attention to his book.

After a while, she remarked, "Miss Eliza Bennet, let me persuade you to follow my example, and take a turn about the room. I assure you it is very refreshing after sitting so long in one attitude."

Darcy, looking up immediately, was awake to the novelty of attention for Miss Elizabeth Bennet from Caroline Bingley, and closed his book. He was directly invited to join their party, but declined, observing that he could imagine but two motives for their choosing to walk up and down the room together, with either of which his joining them would interfere.

"What could he mean?" said Caroline Bingley, and she asked Miss Elizabeth Bennet whether she could at all understand him.

"Not at all," was her answer; "but depend upon it, he means to be severe on us, and our surest way of disappointing him, will be to ask nothing about it."

She looked at Darcy as she spoke, and he thought that there was more than a hint of humour in her eyes.

Miss Bingley, however, was incapable of disappointing Mr. Darcy in anything, and persevered therefore in requiring an explanation of his two motives.

Had Caroline Bingley been alone, Darcy might not have pursued the matter. Since, however, Miss Bennet was involved in the matter, Darcy was only too happy to promote the conversation.

"I have not the smallest objection to explaining them. You either choose this method of passing the evening because you are in each other's confidence and have secret affairs to discuss."

Darcy paused, for this seemed to be less than likely, so he continued, "Or because you are conscious that your figures appear to the greatest advantage in walking. If the first, I should be completely in your way; and if the second, I can admire you much better as I sit by the fire."

"Oh! shocking!" cried Miss Bingley. "I never heard anything so abominable. How shall we punish him for such a speech?"

Darcy waited with expectation for the reply to this, and was intrigued by the answer.

"Nothing so easy, if you have but the inclination," said Miss Elizabeth. "We can all plague and punish one another. Tease him, laugh at him. Intimate as you are, you must know how it is to be done."

"But upon my honour I do not," said Caroline Bingley. "I do assure you that my intimacy has not yet taught me that. Tease calmness of temper and presence of mind! No, no, I feel he may defy us there. And as to laughter, we will not expose ourselves, if you please, by attempting to laugh without a subject. Mr. Darcy may hug himself."

"Mr. Darcy is not to be laughed at!" cried Miss Elizabeth. "That is an uncommon advantage, and uncommon I hope it will continue, for it would be a great loss to me to have many such acquaintance. I dearly love a laugh."

Darcy was not very sure how to take this.

"Miss Bingley," said he, "has given me credit for more than can be. The wisest and the best of men, nay, the wisest and best of their actions, may be rendered ridiculous by a person whose first object in life is a joke."

"Certainly," replied Miss Bennet, "there are such people, but I hope I am not one of them. I hope I never ridicule what is wise or good. Follies and nonsense, whims and inconsistencies do divert me, I own, and I laugh at them whenever I can. But these, I suppose, are precisely what you are without."

Darcy regarded her with more appearance of calm than he felt.

"Perhaps that is not possible for any one. But it has been the study of my life to avoid those weaknesses which often expose a strong understanding to ridicule."

She regarded him for a moment and then said, "Such as vanity and pride?"

"Yes, vanity is a weakness indeed. But pride—where there is a real superiority of mind, pride will be always under good regulation."

Miss Bennet turned away, as if to hide a smile.

"Your examination of Mr. Darcy is over, I presume," said Miss Bingley; "and pray what is the result?"

"I am perfectly convinced by it that Mr. Darcy has no defect," replied Miss Elizabeth. "He owns it himself without disguise."

"No," said Darcy, rather vexed, "I have made no such pretension. I have faults enough, but they are not, I hope, of understanding."

He stopped then, intending to say no more, but his irritation was too much for that to be enough.

"My temper I dare not vouch for. It is I believe too little yielding, certainly too little for the convenience of the world. I cannot forget the follies and vices of others so soon as I ought, nor their offences against myself. My feelings are not puffed about with every attempt to move them."

Then, thinking of his inability to possess Bingley's ease of address in company, and striving to be honest with her without regard to the disbenefit to himself, he added, "My temper would perhaps be called resentful. My good opinion once lost is lost for ever."

"That is a failing indeed!" said Miss Bennet. "Implacable resentment is a shade in a character. But you have chosen your fault well. I really cannot laugh at it. You are safe from me."

Darcy, realising his error, then sought to excuse himself.

"There is, I believe, in every disposition a tendency to some particular evil, a natural defect, which not even the best education can overcome."

If he had known her better, he might have expected that she would not let that rest.

"And your defect is a propensity to hate every body."

"And yours," he replied with a slow smile, "is wilfully to misunderstand them."

"Do let us have a little music," cried Miss Bingley, tired of a conversation in which she had no share, and clearly dissatisfied at being so long overlooked.

"Louisa, you will not mind my walking Mr. Hurst." Her sister made no objection, and the piano-forte was opened.

Darcy, after a few moments' recollection, was not sorry for it, since Miss Bingley's resentment at any attention being paid to Miss Elizabeth Bennet was clear. But he was aware that he was more than susceptible to her, especially when she adopted that teasing tone of address which could so beguile him.

10

When Miss Elizabeth Bennet wrote the next morning to her mother, to ask for the carriage to be sent from Longbourn in the course of the day, the reply came that they could not possibly have it before Tuesday; and that, if Mr. Bingley and his sister pressed them to stay longer, she could spare them very well. However, at length it was settled that they should stay till the following day. Bingley repeatedly tried to persuade Miss Jane Bennet that it would not be safe for her, that she was not enough recovered; but she was firm in accepting the use of his carriage for the next morning.

Darcy was in two minds about this news.

On the one hand, it was welcome intelligence. Elizabeth Bennet would have been at Netherfield for four days. That, for the safety of his heart, was more than long enough, as she attracted him much more than was desirable. In addition, Miss Bingley delighted in being uncivil to her, and more teasing than usual to himself.

On the other hand, he felt more strongly towards her than for any woman before, and he could not keep himself from her company while she was in the same house. But the inferiority of her connections made it impossible to contemplate any future in the relationship.

He therefore resolved that he must not encourage her, and should be particularly careful that no sign of admiration should now escape him until she left Netherfield.

Steady to his purpose, Darcy managed to speak scarcely ten words to her through the whole of Saturday. On the following day, after morning service, the Misses Bennet returned to Longbourn.

It was at least a benefit that Caroline Bingley could no longer trouble him about his admiration of "those fine eyes."

However, that night Darcy did not sleep well. Having resolved to remove the lady from his attention, he found that she persisted even more in his mind. Having decided by the small hours to remove himself from Netherfield at least for long enough to avoid the forthcoming ball, Darcy found himself agreeing at breakfast to be present, and even to assist in part of the discussion about the arrangements. Having concluded that it would be politic to support Miss Bingley when she criticised the deportment, appearance or behaviour of Miss Elizabeth Bennet, he found himself doing exactly the opposite.

In short, he found himself unable to control his own free will for the first time in his life.

Two days later, Darcy rode into Meryton with Bingley. Proceeding up the street, he saw some of the Bennet sisters with a gentleman in clerical garb, talking to officers of the regiment quartered in the town. Miss Elizabeth Bennet was in an animated conversation with a tall officer whose figure seemed to be strangely familiar.

Bingley and Darcy, on distinguishing the ladies of the group, both rode towards them, and began the usual civilities. Bingley told Miss Bennet that he was on his way to Longbourn on purpose to inquire after her health. Darcy corroborated this with a bow, and was beginning to determine not to fix his eyes on Miss Elizabeth Bennet, when his glance was suddenly taken by the sight of the officer to whom she had been speaking—it was George Wickham.

The countenance of both changed colour as their eyes met. Wickham, after a few moments, touched his hat in a salutation which Darcy just deigned to return. In another minute Bingley, without seeming to have noticed what passed, took leave and Darcy was able to ride on with him, his mind in turmoil.

By what vicious stroke of fate was it that the man whom he detested and above all others wished to avoid should be in this part of Hertfordshire? He had thought at Ramsgate that he would never have to encounter Wickham again. And to see him talking to Miss Elizabeth Bennet! Of all the ladies of his acquaintance, why should she have to be in his company and subject to his attentions?

He made little conversation on the way back and, as he entered Netherfield with his friend, it occurred to Darcy that Bingley's invitations to the officers of the regiment to attend the ball would be likely to include Wickham. There appeared to be no way in which his attendance could be avoided, and that was a most unhappy prospect.

❊   ❊   ❊

The following day, Bingley took his sisters to Longbourn to invite the Bennet family to the ball.

Darcy declined to go with them, seeking to avoid any further exposure to Mrs. Bennet.

Although he had not until now acknowledged it to himself, his disdain of dancing had been modified, as far as the forthcoming ball was concerned, by the prospect that he could persuade Miss Elizabeth Bennet to be his partner.

His reluctance at the Meryton assembly to accept Bingley's suggestion to that effect, her refusal to accord with Sir William's proposal at the Lucases, and her rejection of his invitation to dance a reel at Netherfield, were in his mind. It was unusual, to say the least, for Darcy to contemplate with pleasure the company of a lady in the dance. But so it was now.

Against that was now the possibility that she might again refuse him, and that there might be others, including a man whom he heartily disliked and mistrusted, who could also seek her hand for that purpose.

11

As the guests arrived on the day of the Netherfield ball, Darcy stood at the side of the room, a short distance from his hosts as they greeted the company on their arrival. The officers of the regiment arrived together, with Colonel Forster and his young wife. Darcy could not see Wickham amongst them, although he recognised Mr. Denny who had been at the encounter in Meryton a few days earlier.

Darcy had little interest in most of the other arrivals, although he noticed Sir William and Lady Lucas with their two eldest daughters. At last, the Bennet family arrived together, Miss Elizabeth Bennet in lively conversation with her father as they entered the house.

Darcy saw her then accompany her eldest sister into the drawing-room.

He took the opportunity to make a polite enquiry as to how she and her sister were, to which she replied with some civility. As he left her, he noted that she then looked around the room, as though searching for someone among the cluster of the officers in red coats there assembled. Darcy saw Miss Lydia Bennet walk across the room and approach Mr. Denny, who spoke to her and her sister Elizabeth, Denny looking towards Darcy as he did so.

Darcy's reverie was then interrupted by the music starting up, Bingley taking the eldest Miss Bennet onto the floor, and her sister joining the dance with the clerical gentleman who had been with the Bennet family at Meryton. The latter soon proved to be no kind of dancer, often moving wrong without being aware of it. Miss Elizabeth Bennet appeared to be gracious in the face of these difficulties. Darcy was gratified to see that there was very little conversation between them during the two dances. When the music eventually came to an end, the lady appeared to leave the floor with some alacrity.

As he walked around the ballroom, Miss Bingley interrupted his perambulation to tell him that she had overheard one of the officers speaking to Miss Lydia Bennet. The officer had turned to look at Darcy, as he said that "Mr. Wickham had been obliged to go to town on business the day before, although I do not imagine that his business would have called him away just now, if he had not wished to avoid a certain gentleman here."

This intelligence pleased Darcy, since he had no wish to meet Wickham that evening, or indeed at all. But it also implied that all the old falsehoods about the dealings between them were being promoted again in Hertfordshire.

He walked on until he was within a few steps of Miss Elizabeth Bennet, resolving that he must seek his chance now, before her card was filled for the evening. However, for the moment, he was too late, for at that instant she took the floor with one of the officers. Darcy continued to pace around the room for the next half hour until, at last, the music ended, and she crossed the room to join Miss Charlotte Lucas in conversation.

Darcy quickly passed behind the company and, addressing her with few preliminaries, applied for her hand for the next two dances. Miss Bennet hesitated for what seemed to him a long moment. Then she accepted his offer without comment, and he turned away immediately, but with a feeling of satisfaction which he had rarely experienced.

When the dancing recommenced, Miss Lucas and Miss Bennet were deep in conversation as Darcy approached to claim her hand. Together, they took their places opposite each other in the set. He noticed that the nearest of the company seemed to be taking a lively interest in the rare spectacle of his taking to the floor.

As the first couples began the steps, they both stood silent, not speaking a word.

Then, it was their turn. When he took her hand for the first turn, Darcy found himself close to being overcome with feelings that were as powerful as they were novel. Her touch was firm, more steady and confident than that of many women, and her balance was sure as she turned away from him and then back, as the dance required.

He was so little inclined normally to speak whilst dancing that the absence of words to begin with did not bother him. After a few minutes, she made some slight observation on the dance. He replied briefly, and was again silent. It was enough for him for the moment to be where he was, and with her.

After a silence for some minutes, she addressed him a second time.

"It is your turn to say something now, Mr. Darcy. I talked about the dance, and you ought to make some kind of remark on the size of the room, or the number of couples."

This was very unlike the stilted conversation that Darcy was used to on such occasions and, despite himself, he smiled, and assured her that whatever she wished him to say should be said.

She seemed encouraged by this, and said, "Very well. That reply will do for the present. Perhaps bye and bye I may observe that private balls are much pleasanter than public ones. But now we may be silent."

Her confidence commended itself to him.

"Do you talk by rule then, while you are dancing?"

"Sometimes," she replied, "One must speak a little, you know. It would look odd to be entirely silent for half an hour together, and yet for the advantage of some, conversation ought to be so arranged as that they may have the trouble of saying as little as possible."

Again he found himself reflecting that the manner of her address was a refreshing change to that to which he was accustomed.

"Are you consulting your own feelings in the present case, or do you imagine that you are gratifying mine?"

"Both," replied Miss Bennet, "for I have always seen a great similarity in the turn of our minds."

She paused, as his heart warmed to the disclosure that she had given more than a little thought to the subject.

Then she went on to say, slowly, "We are each of an unsocial, taciturn disposition, unwilling to speak, unless we expect to say something that will amaze the whole room, and be handed down to posterity with all the eclat of a proverb."

He was not happy with this response.

"This is no very striking resemblance of your own character, I am sure. How near it may be to mine, I cannot pretend to say."

Then, although unaware that he disclosed some irritation at what might be a criticism of himself, he added, "You think it a faithful portrait undoubtedly."

"I must not decide on my own performance."

He made no answer, and they were again silent till they had gone down the dance.

Recalling how she had reached Netherfield when her sister was ill, and where they had last met, Darcy then asked her cautiously if she and her sisters very often walked the mile from Longbourn to Meryton.

"Yes," she answered and added, "when you met us there the other day, we had just been forming a new acquaintance."

He was immediately aware to whom she referred — Wickham! — and he was aware that the colour came into his face. But he did not reply immediately.

At length he said, in a constrained manner, "Mr. Wickham is blessed with such happy manners as may ensure his making friends. Whether he may be equally capable of retaining them, is less certain."

Darcy was not prepared for the firm reply, which seemed to be based on more than a limited acquaintance between Wickham and Miss Elizabeth Bennet.

"He has been so unlucky as to lose your friendship, and in a manner which he is likely to suffer from all his life."

This reply indicated some measure of intimacy between her and Wickham which concerned Darcy almost beyond reason.

But he made no answer. Indeed, he had none. If he had been feeling more rational, he might have been aware that he was blaming that gentleman for again coming into his life to damage something that mattered to him.

At that moment, Sir William Lucas appeared, seeking to pass through the set to the other side of the room. Seeing them together, he stopped with a bow to compliment him on his dancing and his partner.

"I have been most highly gratified indeed, my dear Sir. Such very superior dancing is not often seen. It is evident that you belong to the first circles. Allow me to say, however, that your fair partner does not disgrace you, and that I must hope to have this pleasure often repeated, especially when a certain desirable event, my dear Miss Eliza, shall take place."

At this point, Darcy saw that Sir William was looking at her sister, Jane Bennet, and Bingley. He was brought back to the present company by Sir William.

"What congratulations will then flow in! I appeal to Mr. Darcy; but let me not interrupt you, Sir. You will not thank me for detaining you from the bewitching converse of that young lady, whose bright eyes are also upbraiding me."

Darcy's attention to the latter part of this address was very limited, as Sir William's allusion to his friend kept his thoughts with Bingley, who was dancing with the eldest Miss Bennet. A novel and unwelcome thought came into Darcy's mind. Was that the general opinion, that his friend and Miss Jane Bennet . . .

However, he recollected himself, and turned to his partner, saying, "Sir William's interruption has made me forget what we were talking of."

She replied, rather sharply he thought, "I do not think we were speaking at all. Sir William could not have interrupted any two people in the room who had less to say for themselves. We have tried two to three subjects already without success, and what we are to talk of next I cannot imagine."

With the dance soon to come to the end, he realised that his opportunity to speak to her again during the evening might be very limited, and he determined to change the subject to something more likely to produce a favourable reply.

Remembering that, like her father, she seemed to be fond of reading, Darcy tried again.

"What think you of books?" said he, smiling.

But she seemed determined not to be pleased.

"Books. Oh! no. I am sure we never read the same, or not with the same feelings."

He tried again, though disappointed at her reaction.

"I am sorry you think so; but if that be the case, there can at least be no want of subject. We may compare our different opinions."

"No. I cannot talk of books in a ball-room; my head is always full of something else."

His confidence in receiving a more sympathetic response was fading.

"The present always occupies you in such scenes does it?" he said, doubtfully this time.

"Yes, always," she replied.

There was silence between them for some time.

Then she suddenly exclaimed, "I remember hearing you once say, Mr. Darcy, that you hardly ever forgave, that your resentment once created was unappeasable. You are very cautious, I suppose, as to its being created."

For several moments, he puzzled as to the reason that might be behind this question, but could not discern it, so he replied, more resolutely than he felt, "I am."

"And never allow yourself to be blinded by prejudice?"

He was genuinely surprised, for the idea had never occurred to him as a possibility.

"I hope not," he replied.

There was a silence again, although more brief this time.

"It is particularly incumbent on those who never change their opinion, to be secure of judging properly at first."

He reflected that it seemed like a query, rather than a statement.

"May I ask to what these questions tend?"

"Merely to the illustration of your character," she said gravely. "I am trying to make it out."

He took some comfort that this remark at least did not indicate any indifference to him and, emboldened, asked her, "And what is your success?"

She shook her head. "I do not get on at all. I hear such different accounts of you as puzzle me exceedingly."

For a moment, he was not at all sure how best to reply. She might, after all, have heard any manner of falsehoods about him from Wickham. With that in mind, he answered seriously.

"I can readily believe, that report may vary greatly with respect to me; and I could wish, Miss Bennet, that you were not to sketch my character at the present moment, as there is reason to fear that the performance would reflect no credit on either."

She looked at him almost anxiously as she said, "But if I do not take your likeness now, I may never have another opportunity."

What meaning this had was not clear to Darcy, and he said to her more coldly, "I would by no means suspend any pleasure of yours."

She said no more, and they went down the dance for the last time. At the end, they parted in silence.

Despite this unsatisfactory ending to the encounter, she had revealed some interest in his own person as to make Darcy not unhappy with her.

His anger was therefore directed solely towards a former acquaintance of his own. Darcy stood apart from the throng as they took the floor again, and regretted every unfortunate consequence of his family's long acquaintance with George Wickham.

At last the time came for everyone to take refreshment. Darcy moved with the rest of the company to the dining room, where a choice of dishes was laid out on the tables.

It was in a disturbed frame of mind that Darcy took his seat at a table. He had scarcely begun to eat when he was accosted by the clerical gentleman who had seemed to be with the party from Longbourn. He was unable to conceal his astonishment as this person prefaced his speech with a solemn bow, and introduced himself as the Bennets' cousin, Mr. Collins, lately engaged by Darcy's aunt, Lady Catherine de Bourgh, as the rector at Hunsford. He then went on, at length, to express his good fortune at obtaining that position, and the consequent opportunity to meet his patron so regularly in the course of his duties.

By this time, Darcy was eyeing him with unrestrained wonder. When at last Mr. Collins allowed him time to speak, he replied with an air of distant civility, saying only that he was so well convinced of Lady Catherine's discernment as to be certain she could never bestow a favour unworthily.

Mr. Collins, however, was not to be discouraged.

Instead, he carried on speaking again, although mostly by repetition of what he had already expounded. Finally, Darcy mustered a slight bow, and was able to move away to fetch a glass of wine.

When he returned to his place, he was not pleased to find that Mrs. Bennet had taken her seat opposite him with Lady Lucas, with whom she was talking loudly. More welcome was the realisation that Miss Elizabeth Bennet was sitting at the same table, although also opposite himself and much too far away for him to make any conversation.

He was unable to avoid hearing the exchange between Mrs. Bennet and Lady Lucas, and paid that more attention, as the former seemed to be talking of nothing but her expectation that Miss Jane Bennet would be soon married to Bingley. She seemed incapable of fatigue while enumerating the advantages of the match, his wealth and the benefits to her, as the marriage must throw her younger daughters in the way of other rich men.

Darcy soon became acutely aware of Miss Elizabeth's embarrassment and endeavours to put a stop to her mother's words, or to persuade her to describe her felicity in a less audible manner.

Mrs. Bennet, however, scolded her for being nonsensical,

saying loudly enough for Darcy to hear, "What is Mr. Darcy to me, pray, that I should be afraid of him? I am sure we owe him no such particular civility as to be obliged to say nothing he may not like to hear."

"For heaven's sake, madam, speak lower," he heard Miss Elizabeth Bennet say. "What advantage can it be to you to offend Mr. Darcy? You will never recommend yourself to his friend by so doing."

This had no effect, Mrs. Bennet continuing in the same vein.

Darcy tried when he could to look elsewhere, for he was aware of the daughter glancing towards him when she thought that she was not observed, but he missed very little of what was being said to Lady Lucas. Everything that he heard confirmed his previous view that Mrs. Bennet was vulgar, thoughtless, ill-mannered and the last person in the world whom Bingley should desire as a mother-in-law.

In that, Darcy reflected, he profoundly shared Miss Bingley's opinion. And Mrs. Bennet's younger daughters appeared to possess little sense, and even less decorum in company, and few accomplishments of which they might be proud. Indeed, they were a very unhappy contrast to the modest demeanour of his sister Georgiana and the talents of other ladies of his acquaintance.

At last Mrs. Bennet had no more to say, but the respite for Darcy was short.

As supper was now over, Bingley invited those prepared to oblige the company to sing. Before others had the opportunity, Miss Mary Bennet accepted this invitation with alacrity. The performance was to Darcy no comparison to that of Miss Elizabeth, whom he had heard playing at previous gatherings in Meryton. At last, the young lady was prevailed upon by her father, in a manner that reminded Darcy a little of his second daughter, to give way.

At this moment, the voice of the rector of Hunsford, Mr. Collins, was again heard.

"If I," said Mr. Collins, "were so fortunate as to be able to sing, I should have great pleasure, I am sure, in obliging the company with an air; for I consider music as a very innocent diversion, and perfectly compatible with the profession of a clergyman. I do not mean however to assert that we can be justified in devoting too much of our time to music, for there are certainly other things to be attended to. The rector of a parish has much to do. In the first place, he must make such an agreement for tithes as may be beneficial to himself and not offensive to his patron. He must write his own sermons; and the time that remains will not be too much for his parish duties, and the care and improvement of his dwelling, which he cannot be excused from making as comfortable as possible. And I do not think it of light importance that he should have attentive and conciliatory manners towards every body, especially towards those to whom he owes his preferment. I cannot acquit him of that duty, nor could I think well of the man who should omit an occasion of testifying his respect towards anybody connected with the family."

And with a bow to Mr. Darcy, he concluded his speech, which had been spoken so loud as to be heard by half the room.

Mr. Bennet looked amused, but his wife commended Mr. Collins for having spoken so sensibly, and observed in a half-whisper to Lady Lucas that he was a remarkably clever, good kind of young man. Darcy said nothing, but he had no difficulty in taking a different view.

At that moment, Miss Bingley appeared by Darcy's side.

"I have been having a fascinating conversation with a lady whom I know you favour. It seems that she is so persuaded of the attractions of a certain Mr. Wickham that she does not wish to listen to well-intentioned advice from someone as independent of the matter as myself. They would make a pretty pair, would they not, Mr. Darcy, she and Mr. Wickham? Indeed, you must agree that they seem to be made for each other."

These remarks put Darcy into such a bad humour that for once he was glad of an intervention from Sir William, who at that moment came up to compliment Bingley and his sister on the excellence of their arrangements for the ball.

The remainder of the evening passed with little incident, and nothing to please Darcy. He had some conversation with Mr. Bennet about the library at Pemberley, which the latter gentleman had heard was very fine. Darcy noticed that Mr. Bennet came alive when in discourse on the subject of reading and books, and their conversation at least passed some minutes of the evening. A few comments that Mr. Bennet let slip indicated that he regarded Mr. Collins, on whom the estate at Longbourn was apparently entailed after his death, as a source of considerable amusement, and not as a man of any great intelligence or good sense. This was not a view with which it was difficult for Darcy to concur.

The clergyman appeared to be exceptionally attentive to Miss Elizabeth, who danced no more and sat out at the side of the room. That they were joined by Miss Charlotte Lucas, Darcy noticed, seemed to be very welcome to her friend.

Darcy could find nothing other to do than to spend the remainder of the evening standing within a very short distance of them, having no interest in dancing with anyone else in the room. Meanwhile, Bingley continued his attentions to the eldest Miss Bennet.

On the following day, Darcy knew, Bingley was due to travel to town on business. He resolved to have a serious talk with his friend's sisters in his absence. The situation between Bingley and Miss Bennet had clearly developed much further than he had anticipated, and something needed to be done.

Part Three

Darcy had never been so bewitched by any woman as he was by her.

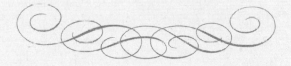

12

Some seven days later, Darcy reviewed the events of the past week with satisfaction.

After Bingley had left for town, his friend had soon discovered that his disdain at the behaviour of much of the Longbourn party at the ball was endorsed and exceeded by both Miss Bingley and Mrs. Hurst. However pleasant the manners of the eldest Miss Bennet, it was agreed that the rest of her family, and in particular her mother and three youngest sisters, were quite inappropriate connections for a family of Bingley's consequence. Any partiality that Charles might feel for Miss Jane Bennet could surely evaporate as rapidly as his enthusiasm for other young ladies had done in the past.

Following their discussion, Darcy had travelled himself to London with Miss Bingley and Mr. and Mrs. Hurst. It had been agreed during the journey that Bingley should be persuaded by his friend of the indifference of Miss Jane Bennet, which indeed had seemed to that gentleman to be the case from his observance of her. Miss Bingley could not resist inserting a barb about Miss Elizabeth's "fine eyes" in the conversation, but Darcy chose to ignore this. In the privacy of his room, he had reflected that any objections that applied to the eldest Miss Bennet having any alliance with his friend were more than magnified and reinforced in the view of his own greater consequence and fortune.

In the event, Darcy was a little surprised that the task of persuading Bingley that he should remain in London was not accomplished easily.

His friend was usually more willing to accept his advice and direction than now appeared in this case. Bingley seemed to be persuaded that his feelings were stronger and persistent than on previous occasions, and less susceptible to being eradicated by time. However, by dint of repeating Darcy's and his sisters' conviction many times that the lady's affections were not engaged, over a period of days Bingley was also convinced of his own indifference.

If it then seemed in the ensuing weeks that his friend was at times more pensive and reflective than was his habit, Darcy did not allow that to concern him.

There was one short alarm, when Miss Bingley told Darcy that she had had a formal call from Miss Jane Bennet. It appeared that she had travelled to London to stay for some weeks with those same relations in Cheapside of which so much sport had been made in Miss Bingley's conversation in Hertfordshire.

However, although the call was eventually returned, the news of the visitor from Longbourn being in town was kept from Charles Bingley. Darcy could therefore contemplate with some satisfaction the way that his friend's temporary affliction of the heart had been dealt with.

❀   ❀   ❀

What did surprise Darcy was the obstinate difficulty he himself had in removing from his own mind the image of Miss Elizabeth Bennet during the next few weeks in town.

Darcy in his youth had spent the festive season at Pemberley, and it had been his happiest time of year in the company of his parents. Since their demise, Darcy had avoided Derbyshire until the weather at the end of the winter made the roads more fit to travel, after the January snows.

But he could not recall when he had suffered such an uneasy mind. The more he sought, as the New Year began, to eliminate Miss Elizabeth Bennet from his thoughts and interest, the less he seemed to succeed. Making more effort than usual to encounter other company in town had no countervailing effect. The society of ladies of his own consequence only seemed to provoke memories of lively conversation and pleasant and more informed wit from that other source.

Indeed, his failure to thus control his thoughts made him more abrupt than was in any case his habit. He found himself particularly short of temper in company with Miss Caroline Bingley. Her wit, which he had once found pleasantly astringent and barbed, now seemed particularly affected and tiresome. His sister's joining him in London for once offered only some assistance in this situation.

However, to keep himself occupied, he took Georgiana to seek some new furniture for her sitting room, and had some pleasure in her delight at the opportunity. By such minor pursuits, Darcy passed the next few weeks. The prospect of any relief from the tedium of the season in town was small, and the most exciting excursion that the future promised was his annual visit for about ten days after

Easter with Colonel Fitzwilliam to his aunt, Lady Catherine, in Kent.

This was not something to which Darcy normally looked forward. Fitzwilliam's company could be had elsewhere with greater pleasure, his cousin Anne had little to recommend her, and Lady Catherine made such forceful discourse, with her own replies, as to make it even less necessary than usual for Darcy to persuade himself to make polite conversation.

The prospect of the tiresome new rector, Mr. Collins, being added to the company from time to time was no additional inducement on its own.

However, a communication from his aunt brought the surprising news that Mr. Collins had returned from his most recent visit to Hertfordshire after the Christmas festival with a bride—none other than Charlotte, the eldest daughter of Sir William Lucas.

Darcy had regarded Miss Lucas as one of the more sensible and serious young ladies he had met while at Netherfield. More significant was that she was a close friend of Miss Elizabeth Bennet. As March began, and the time of his visit drew nearer, he was aware that he would welcome the opportunity to hear some news from the new Mrs. Collins of a young lady from another county.

Then a second letter came from his aunt. Together with the usual advice to himself about Georgiana, it informed him that none other than Miss Elizabeth Bennet herself was at the parsonage at Hunsford, accompanying Miss Maria Lucas on a visit to her sister. However, their stay of some six weeks would end just before Darcy and Fitzwilliam were due to arrive in Kent.

Almost before he knew what he had done, Darcy had

written a swift note to his cousin Fitzwilliam, who was in the
north for a few weeks before travelling to town.

His cousin's reply came by return on Friday.

> *"Dear Darcy*
>
> *Your enthusiasm for travelling to Kent to see our aunt*
> *is most commendable. I shall, as you ask, arrange to be*
> *in town three weeks earlier than we agreed, so that we can*
> *be at Rosings in time for Easter. Forgive this short note —*
> *written in haste.*
>
> *James Fitzwilliam."*

Darcy wrote to his aunt to say that he planned to arrive
for his visit to Kent in the week before the festival, and received a letter within a few days welcoming the idea.

His cousin reached London in time for them to leave for
Kent some eight days before Easter. On the journey from
town, Fitzwilliam asked Darcy how he had been passing his
time since they last met. Darcy, without naming his friend,
recounted his success in separating Bingley from an unfortunate alliance that could have damaged his situation for life.
He took pains to emphasise that his motives had been allied
with the knowledge that the affections of neither of the parties had been fully engaged, and so that the whole affair had
been for the best.

Fitzwilliam commended Darcy for his foresight and
rapid action, saying that, as the younger son of an Earl, he
would need to have regard to fortune and position himself
when he married. His cousin added that, now that he had attained his thirtieth year, marriage was a matter to which
Fitzwilliam might need to give some more serious attention.

13

Thus it was that Darcy and his cousin arrived in Kent at the beginning of April, with Easter only a few days away.

He had apprised Fitzwilliam that there might be more enjoyable company than usual awaiting them at Rosings. On the day after their arrival, the rector Mr. Collins arrived to pay his respects. Darcy found him in every way as curious and pompous as he had at Netherfield the previous autumn.

However, having had a few hours in the company of Lady Catherine and their cousin Anne the previous evening, Fitzwilliam needed little persuading to walk back with Darcy to the parsonage in Hunsford with Mr. Collins, to pay their respects to the rector's new wife and her visitors. Their approach having been announced by the door-bell, Darcy and his cousin found the former Miss Charlotte Lucas a pleasant contrast to her husband's verbosity.

Her younger sister, Maria, and Miss Elizabeth Bennet

curtseyed to the visitors, but said nothing on the introduction to Darcy himself.

Darcy ventured a compliment to Mrs. Collins on the
house and garden, but was more interested to listen to the
conversation between his cousin and her friend. The latter
seemed to Darcy to be much as he remembered her, as his
cousin's ease of address and ready manner led Miss Bennet
into conversation with him. Her lively manner and sense of
humour were soon displayed, and he found himself en-
grossed in their discussion.

At length, however, Darcy enquired of Miss Bennet
about the health of her family. She answered him in the
usual way, and then added "My eldest sister has been in
town these three months. Have you never happened to see
her there?"

Darcy was uneasily aware of his own embarrassment as
he answered that he had never been so fortunate as to meet
Miss Bennet. The subject was pursued no further, and
Darcy soon made his excuses and went away with
Fitzwilliam.

Over the next few days, his cousin called at the parsonage several times, but Darcy refused to join him, jealous that
Fitzwilliam's more easy manners would show his own at a
disadvantage. As a consequence, he was only able to glimpse
Miss Bennet at church.

However, no sooner had Darcy been pleased to find that
his aunt did not intend to see much of Mr. and Mrs. Collins
whilst her nephews were staying, than he found himself
wishing the opposite, so that he could encounter one of their
visitors.

However, it took several carefully placed suggestions to

bring it about that, by Easter-day, almost a week after his arrival, an invitation was issued for the party from Hunsford to spend the evening at Rosings after leaving church.

Mr. and Mrs. Collins with their guests joined Lady Catherine's party in the drawing room. Her ladyship, however, gave them little attention, speaking to her nephews and especially to Darcy, much more than to any other person in the room.

However, Fitzwilliam seemed really glad to see them; since anything was a welcome relief to him at Rosings; and Mrs. Collins's pretty friend, Miss Bennet, seemed to have caught his fancy. Thus he sat by her, talking agreeably of Kent and Hertfordshire, of travelling and staying at home, of new books and music, so that Miss Bennet gave Darcy the appearance of having never been half so well entertained in that room before. He himself was full of feelings that, if they had been more familiar, would have been recognised as jealousy.

She and his cousin conversed with so much spirit and flow, as to draw the attention of Lady Catherine herself, as well as that of Darcy. Lady Catherine was more visibly put out at not being the centre of attention as she was used to, and she called out to his cousin.

"What is that you are saying, Fitzwilliam? What is it you are talking of? What are you telling Miss Bennet? Let me hear what it is."

"We are speaking of music, Madam," said he, making a resigned face to Darcy, when no longer able to avoid a reply.

"Of music! Then pray speak aloud. It is of all subjects my delight. I must have my share in the conversation, if you are speaking of music. There are few people in England, I suppose, who have more true enjoyment of music than myself, or a better natural taste. If I had ever learnt, I should have been a great proficient. And so would Anne, if her health had allowed her to apply. I am confident that she would have performed delightfully."

Then turning to Darcy, she continued, "How does Georgiana get on?"

"She is most competent for her age, Madam, and practices as often as she can."

"I am very glad to hear such a good account of her," said Lady Catherine; "and pray tell her from me, that she cannot expect to excel, if she does not practise a great deal."

"I assure you, Madam," he replied, "that she does not need such advice. She practises very constantly."

"So much the better. It cannot be done too much; and when I next write to her, I shall charge her not to neglect it on any account. I often tell young ladies, that no excellence in music is to be acquired, without constant practise."

"I have told Miss Bennet several times, that she will never play really well, unless she practises more; and though Mrs. Collins has no instrument, she is very welcome, as I have often told her, to come to Rosings every day, and play on the piano forte in Mrs. Jenkinson's room. She would be in nobody's way, you know, in that part of the house."

Darcy did not answer, since even a man of his consequence could recognise the incivility of this remark.

When coffee was over, Fitzwilliam reminded Miss Bennet of having promised to play to him. As she sat down directly to the instrument, he drew a chair near her. Darcy would have joined them, but was detained by his aunt for many minutes. Eventually, she was distracted by a conversation with Mr. Collins, and Darcy was able to move away and join his cousin so as to observe Miss Bennet at the pianoforte.

At the first convenient pause, she turned to him with a smile, and said,

"You mean to frighten me, Mr. Darcy, by coming in all this state to hear me? But I will not be alarmed though your sister does play so well. There is a stubbornness about me that never can bear to be frightened at the will of others. My courage always rises with every attempt to intimidate me."

Darcy was cheered by this reversion to the playful manner in which she had sometimes addressed him in Hertfordshire.

"I shall not say that you are mistaken," he replied, "because you could not really believe me to entertain any design of alarming you; and I have had the pleasure of your acquaintance long enough to know, that you find great enjoyment in occasionally professing opinions which in fact are not your own."

Miss Bennet laughed at this picture of herself, and said to Fitzwilliam, "Your cousin will give you a very pretty notion of me, and teach you not to believe a word I say. I am particularly unlucky in meeting with a person so well able to expose my real character, in a part of the world, where I had hoped to pass myself off with some degree of credit."

Then turning back to Darcy, she said,

"Indeed, Mr. Darcy, it is very ungenerous in you to mention all that you knew to my disadvantage in Hertfordshire and, give me leave to say, very impolitic too, for it is provoking me to retaliate, and such things may come out, as will shock your relations to hear."

This reply and manner of speaking stirred in him feelings that were familiar, and far from unwelcome.

"I am not afraid of you," said he, with good humour.

"Pray let me hear what you have to accuse him of," cried Fitzwilliam. "I should like to know how he behaves among strangers."

Darcy awaited her next words with little apprehension, since she had smiled at him again, and that was worth any degree of discomfort that he was likely to suffer.

"You shall hear then, but prepare yourself for something very dreadful," said Miss Bennet. "The first time of my ever seeing him in Hertfordshire, you must know, was at a ball, and at this ball, what do you think he did? He danced only four dances! I am sorry to pain you, but so it was. He danced only four dances, though gentlemen were scarce; and, to my certain knowledge, more than one young lady was sitting down in want of a partner. Mr. Darcy, you cannot deny the fact."

Darcy's mind went back immediately to the assembly at Meryton, and his rejection of Bingley's suggestion that he should dance with Miss Elizabeth. In his embarrassment, he replied rather stiffly.

"I had not at that time the honour of knowing any lady in the assembly beyond my own party."

"True; and nobody can ever be introduced in a ballroom." She smiled again at Darcy, before turning to his cousin.

"Well, Colonel Fitzwilliam, what do I play next? My fingers wait your orders."

However, Darcy intervened, for he was more than reluctant to lose her attention.

"Perhaps," he said, "I should have judged better, had I

sought an introduction, but I am ill qualified to recommend myself to strangers."

"Shall we ask your cousin the reason of this?" said Miss Bennet, still addressing his cousin Fitzwilliam. "Shall we ask him why a man of sense and education, and who has lived in the world, is ill qualified to recommend himself to strangers?"

"I can answer your question," said Fitzwilliam, "without applying to him. It is because he will not give himself the trouble."

"I certainly have not the talent which some people possess," said Darcy, "of conversing easily with those I have never seen before. I cannot catch their tone of conversation, or appear interested in their concerns, as I often see done."

"My fingers," said Miss Bennet, "do not move over this instrument in the masterly manner which I see so many women's do. They have not the same force or rapidity, and do not produce the same expression. But then I have always supposed it to be my own fault, because I would not take the trouble of practising. It is not that I do not believe my fingers as capable as any other woman's of superior execution."

Darcy smiled, for there was no denying the justice of her remark.

"You are perfectly right. You have employed your time much better. No one admitted to the privilege of hearing you, can think anything wanting."

He hesitated for a moment, and then added, "We neither of us perform to strangers."

He would have wished to continue the conversation further, but they were interrupted, as Lady Catherine called out to know of what they were talking.

Miss Bennet immediately began playing again as Lady

Catherine approached, and, after listening for a few minutes, his aunt said to Darcy,

"Miss Bennet would not play at all amiss, if she practised more, and could have the advantage of a London master. She has a very good notion of fingering, though her taste is not equal to Anne's. Anne would have been a delightful performer, had her health allowed her to learn."

Lady Catherine continued her remarks on Miss Bennet's performance, mixing with them many more instructions. Darcy looked at the lady to see how she took this and the comments that followed on playing the instrument, but the performer received them with forbearance. At the request of the gentlemen, she remained at the instrument till her ladyship's carriage was ready to take the party home to Hunsford.

When their aunt had retired for the night, Fitzwilliam remarked to his cousin, "Miss Bennet seems to bring out the best in you, Darcy! I have rarely seen you as animated in company as you were tonight."

"You did not seem indifferent yourself," said Darcy, seeking to redirect his cousin's attention. "But remember, Fitzwilliam, that she comes from a family with no fortune, and very limited connections."

"She is not for me, you mean," said his cousin regretfully. "But you are right, the younger son of an Earl must marry for money. At least, that consideration need not worry you, Darcy."

"You imagine more than there is."

"I hope so," Fitzwilliam replied, "for I have a strong impression that our aunt has other plans in mind for you and, as we both know, she likes to have her own way."

To this, Darcy thought it wise to make no reply.

~ 14 ~

The following morning, Darcy went for a walk in the woods to the north of Rosings. Despite himself, and contrary to any intention of which he was consciously aware, after another half an hour he found himself ringing the bell at the parsonage.

To his surprise, the other two ladies were absent in the village, and he found Miss Bennet alone, writing a letter.

Having been invited to sit, he found this uncomfortable. On standing, he walked about the room, but was not at ease and, without his cousin Fitzwilliam to provide conversation, he found that he had little to say.

At last, Miss Bennet made some enquiries after the family at Rosings.

Then, they again seemed in danger of sinking into total silence. Finally, Miss Bennet said, "How very suddenly you all quitted Netherfield last November, Mr. Darcy! It must have been a most agreeable surprise to Mr. Bingley to see you all after him so soon; for, if I recollect right, he went but the day before."

She paused as though for a reply, but he could think of none, painfully aware that he was not best at untruths, and unable to formulate anything that might not compromise his role in the matter.

At length, she went on, "He and his sisters were well, I hope, when you left London."

Awkwardly he said, "Perfectly so, I thank you."

After a short pause, she added, "I think I have understood that Mr. Bingley has not much idea of ever returning to Netherfield again?"

Darcy replied, "I have never heard him say so."

But then not wishing to imply any intention by Bingley of renewing his friendship with Miss Jane Bennet, Darcy went on, "But it is probable that he may spend very little of his time there in future. He has many friends, and he is at a time of life when friends and engagements are continually increasing."

He found it difficult to gauge her expression as she said, "If he means to be but little at Netherfield, it would be better for the neighbourhood that he should give up the place entirely, for then we might possibly get a settled family there. But perhaps Mr. Bingley did not take the house so much for the convenience of the neighbourhood as for his own, and we must expect him to keep or quit it on the same principle."

"I should not be surprised," said Darcy, "if he were to give it up, as soon as any eligible purchaser offers."

She made no answer.

After a further silence, Darcy tried to make some other conversation.

"This seems a very comfortable house. Lady Catherine, I

believe, did a great deal to it when Mr. Collins first came to Hunsford."

"I believe she did, and I am sure she could not have bestowed her kindness on a more grateful object." She smiled a little at last as she said this.

He tried to continue the conversation by referring to her friend.

"Mr. Collins appears very fortunate in his choice of a wife."

"Yes, indeed; his friends may well rejoice in his having met with one of the very few sensible women who would have accepted him, or have made him happy if they had. My friend has an excellent understanding, though I am not certain that I consider her marrying Mr. Collins as the wisest thing she ever did. She seems perfectly happy, however, and in a prudential light, it is certainly a very good match for her."

Almost without knowing what he said, he went on,

"It must be very agreeable to her to be settled within so easy a distance of her own family and friends."

"An easy distance do you call it? It is nearly fifty miles."

"And what is fifty miles of good road? Little more than half a day's journey," Darcy replied. "Yes, I call it a very easy distance."

She seemed determined not to agree with him. "I should never have considered the distance as one of the advantages of the match. I should never have said Mrs. Collins was settled near her family."

With the distance from Hertfordshire to Pemberley suddenly in his mind, he pressed on, "It is a proof of your own attachment to Hertfordshire. Any thing beyond the very neighbourhood of Longbourn, I suppose, would appear far."

He thought that she might have similar thoughts in her mind, as she blushed as she answered, "I do not mean to say that a woman may not be settled too near her family. The far and the near must be relative, and depend on many varying circumstances. Where there is fortune to make the expense of travelling unimportant, distance becomes no evil."

Darcy was much encouraged by this, for Miss Bennet must be contemplating his own interest in her, and the possibility of her living in Derbyshire.

However, she recollected that they had been speaking of Mrs. Collins, and so returned to speaking about her friend's circumstances.

"But that is not the case here. Mr. and Mrs. Collins have a comfortable income, but not such a one as will allow of frequent journeys, and I am persuaded my friend would not call herself near her family under less than half the present distance."

Anxious to be certain that a distance from Hertfordshire would not be uncongenial, Darcy drew his chair a little towards her, and said, "You cannot have a right to such very strong local attachment. You cannot have been always at Longbourn."

She looked very surprised at this, but said nothing. Darcy drew back his chair, took a newspaper from the table, and, glancing over it, changed the subject by asking,

"Are you pleased with Kent?"

They had maintained more successfully a short dialogue on the subject of that county when Mrs. Collins and her sister entered the room, just returned from their walk.

After greeting them, and sitting a few minutes longer without saying much more, Darcy went away.

15

Despite any intention he had promised to himself, Darcy took every opportunity over the next few days to visit the parsonage, but as often as he could in the company of others.

The season for all field sports was over. Within Rosings, there was Lady Catherine, books, and a billiard table, but the nearness of the parsonage was a temptation almost every day. Darcy and Fitzwilliam called at various times of the morning, sometimes separately, sometimes together, and occasionally with their aunt.

When he was there, Darcy found it no easier to make conversation than on his previous visits to Hunsford. He frequently sat there ten minutes together, cursing his lack of ease in making conversation, and therefore often without opening his lips. But anything was better than not being in her presence and, when he thought that he was not observed, he looked at Miss Bennet. He was aware that the more often he was in her company, the greater his need for it.

Darcy was encouraged by Miss Bennet telling him which were her frequent haunts in the park, believing this to indicate that their encounters were welcome, that she was aware of his interest and was of the same mind about their acquaintance. With the weather being fine for the time of year, and knowing her fondness for walking, he then took pains to cross the paths when he could anticipate that she might be there. Often when they met thus, he would turn back with her towards Hunsford.

When the opportunity offered, he asked Miss Bennet about her love of solitary walks, her pleasure in being at the parsonage with her friend, and her opinion of Mr. and Mrs. Collins's happiness. Later, he risked venturing a question to test whether she might see herself as staying at Rosings on her next visit to Kent.

Thus the days passed quickly, and so much more pleasantly for him than was usual when staying with his aunt, and twice, to his cousin Fitzwilliam's surprise, he postponed their departure from Rosings.

Although Darcy had evinced no more interest than usual in her daughter, on the second occasion that he extended their stay, Lady Catherine evidently thought that his remaining at Rosings indicated that he now had serious intentions towards Anne.

By now, he knew that nothing could be further from the truth. What Darcy had finally come to realise was that without Elizabeth Bennet as his wife, life would no longer be supportable. He had marshalled in his mind every argument against her, against their marriage, recited to himself every objection to her mother, her younger sisters, her aunt in Meryton, her uncle in Cheapside, and all the other inferiorities of her connections. Indeed, he had spent much of the last few nights in restless dispute with himself. But nothing had come to matter to him but his affection, his admiration, his passion for her.

Darcy was acutely aware that his twice postponed departure from Rosings was now imminent, if only because his cousin had business in town, and he himself had promised Georgiana that he would join her within the week. They therefore must leave Kent on Saturday.

The arguments against an alliance between his friend Bingley and Miss Jane Bennet must apply with even more force in his case. But Darcy's resolve to maintain a distance from his feelings of passion and attachment to Elizabeth Bennet had proved to be unsuccessful. Whatever proper considerations of position and propriety might indicate, he now was unable to contemplate a future time that did not include her as the mistress of Pemberley. He had at last to admit to himself that his heart was so engaged that nothing less than a declaration of his affections would do, with the agreement to his suit that would surely follow.

That his proposal might not be successful did not enter his consideration. It would be a rare lady of fashion who would turn down such an offer, however great her fortune. For someone whose father's means were small and whose mother's social position was at best doubtful, it was not conceivable.

Darcy was very aware that he must now find an opportunity to speak to Miss Bennet alone. That might not be an easy task, since she was usually in company with her friend Mrs. Collins or with Miss Lucas. It would be unwise to rely on encountering her in the park, regularly though Miss Bennet might walk there for her own pleasure.

But the circumstances favoured him.

On the Thursday afternoon, Mr. Collins and his party were invited by Lady Catherine to take tea with her. However, when they entered Rosings, it was for Mr. Collins to express abject regret that Miss Bennet had remained at Hunsford, as she was feeling unwell. His aunt seemed to be indifferent to this news, although his cousin Fitzwilliam expressed his regret.

Darcy however determined to have some excuse to leave the company, and did so, making the reason his need to write a letter to his sister.

His feelings of anxiety as he slipped out of the house that afternoon were not based on any apprehensions that his application to Miss Bennet might be rejected.

They related, first, to the fact that she might not be well enough to receive him.

Secondly, Darcy had never flattered himself that he had the ease of manner and happy address of his friend Bingley, or indeed his cousin Fitzwilliam.

He had therefore considered carefully the manner in which he would make clear the force of his affections, and that they had overcome all the obstacles of his position that indicated that he should look elsewhere for his wife.

16

On arriving at the parsonage, he was told that Miss Bennet was in the parlour, and he entered to find her sitting by the window. In an hurried manner he immediately began an enquiry after her health, imputing his visit to a wish of hearing that she was better.

She answered him briefly.

Darcy sat down for a few moments at her invitation, but could not feel easy thus, and so rose and walked about the room for several minutes, seeking as he did so for the right way to begin.

Finally he turned towards her, and was still conscious of his agitation as he spoke.

"In vain have I struggled. It will not do. My feelings will not be repressed. You must allow me to tell you how ardently I admire and love you."

The colour ran from her face and as quickly returned, as she remained silent.

This was not the reaction that he had expected, for he assumed that she had been aware of the special attentions he had been paying to her during his stay in Kent. However, he considered her silence sufficient encouragement to continue, and went on to avow all the affection and attachment in his heart, which he had long felt for her.

However, in fairness to himself, he went on to add his sense of her inferiority, of its being a degradation, of the family obstacles that his judgement had always opposed to inclination.

He concluded with representing to her the strength of that attachment that, in spite of all his endeavours, he had found impossible to conquer; and with expressing his hope that it would now be rewarded by her acceptance of his hand.

He then confidently awaited her answer.

The effect of his words was quite contrary to what he had expected. The colour rose into her cheeks, and she began to speak in terms of angry emotion.

"In such cases as this, it is, I believe, the established mode to express a sense of obligation for the sentiments avowed, however unequally they may be returned. It is natural that obligation should be felt, and if I could feel gratitude, I would now thank you."

"But I cannot—I have never desired your good opinion, and you have certainly bestowed it most unwillingly. I am sorry to have occasioned pain to any one. It has been most unconsciously done, however, and I hope will be of short duration."

Darcy looked at her with disbelief as she continued.

"The feelings which, you tell me, have long prevented the

acknowledgement of your regard, can have little difficulty in overcoming it after this explanation."

Darcy struggled to retain his composure, although his complexion became pale with anger. He tried not to speak until he felt that he was in control of what he should reply, although the disturbance of his mind was visible in every feature.

At length, when he had mastered himself, he said,

"And this is all the reply which I am to have the honour of expecting! I might, perhaps, wish to be informed why, with so little endeavour at civility, I am thus rejected."

He added, although indeed with little truth, "But it is of small importance."

"I might as well enquire," replied she, "why with so evident a design of offending and insulting me, you chose to tell me that you liked me against your will, against your reason, and even against your character? Was not this some excuse for incivility, if I was uncivil?"

For a moment he thought that she had done, but she then continued on quite a different subject.

"But I have other provocations. You know I have. Had not my own feelings decided against you, had they been indifferent, or had they even been favourable, do you think that any consideration would tempt me to accept the man, who has been the means of ruining, perhaps for ever, the happiness of a most beloved sister?"

Darcy was aware that he changed colour as she spoke, for she obviously referred to his influence on Bingley after they had returned from Hertfordshire the previous November. But the reaction was short, and he listened without attempting to interrupt her while she continued.

"I have every reason in the world to think ill of you. No motive can excuse the unjust and ungenerous part you acted there. You dare not, you cannot deny that you have been the principal, if not the only means of dividing them from each other, of exposing one to the censure of the world for caprice and instability, the other to its derision for disappointed hopes, and involving them both in misery of the acutest kind."

She paused; he was silent.

"Can you deny that you have done it?" she repeated.

He took a deep breath before saying, with assumed tranquillity,

"I have no wish of denying that I did every thing in my power to separate my friend from your sister, or that I rejoice in my success."

After a moment's reflection, he went on, "Towards him I have been kinder than towards myself."

She ignored this, as she continued on to another subject much more sensitive as far as he was concerned,

"But it is not merely this affair," she continued, "on which my dislike is founded. Long before it had taken place, my opinion of you was decided. Your character was unfolded in the recital which I received many months ago from Mr. Wickham."

Darcy listened with increasing dismay, as she said,

"On this subject, what can you have to say? In what imaginary act of friendship can you here defend yourself? Or under what misrepresentation, can you here impose upon others?"

Darcy could not help replying angrily,

"You take an eager interest in that gentleman's concerns."

She came back at him immediately,

"Who that knows what his misfortunes have been, can help feeling an interest in him?"

"His misfortunes!" repeated Darcy contemptuously; "yes, his misfortunes have been great indeed."

"And of your infliction," cried Miss Bennet. "You have reduced him to his present state of poverty, comparative poverty. You have withheld the advantages, which you must know to have been designed for him. You have deprived the best years of his life, of that independence which was no less his due than his desert. You have done all this! and yet you can treat the mention of his misfortunes with contempt and ridicule."

Her remarks confirmed Darcy's worst fears of her partiality for Wickham, which he had hoped to have misinterpreted at the ball at Netherfield. "And this," he cried, beginning to lose control over his temper as he walked with quick steps across the room, "is your opinion of me! This is the estimation in which you hold me! I thank you for explaining it so fully. My faults, according to this calculation, are heavy indeed!"

Then a thought occurred to him and, pausing before he crossed the room again in his agitation, he said as he turned towards her, "But perhaps these offences might have been overlooked, had not your pride been hurt by my honest confession of the scruples that had long prevented my forming any serious design."

"These bitter accusations might have been suppressed, had I with greater policy concealed my struggles, and flattered you into the belief of my being impelled by unqualified, unalloyed inclination; by reason, by reflection, by everything."

Darcy looked to her for a reply, but received none. He therefore decided to speak plainly, and said, "But disguise of every sort is my abhorrence. Nor am I ashamed of the feelings I related. They were natural and just. Could you expect me to rejoice in the inferiority of your connections? To congratulate myself on the hope of relations, whose condition in life is so decidedly beneath my own?"

If he had thought to get her agreement on this, he was mistaken, for Miss Bennet rounded on him and replied, "You are mistaken, Mr. Darcy, if you suppose that the mode of your declaration affected me in any other way, than as it spared me the concern which I might have felt in refusing you, had you behaved in a more gentleman-like manner."

Darcy for once was quite dumbfounded, and unable to say anything as she continued, "You could not have made me the offer of your hand in any possible way that would have tempted me to accept it."

Sentiments so opposite to those which he had expected to hear led Darcy to regard her with feelings of mingled incredulity and mortification. But worse was to come.

"From the very beginning, from the first moment I may almost say, of my acquaintance with you, your manners impressing me with the fullest belief of your arrogance, your conceit, and your selfish disdain of the feelings of others, were such as to form that ground-work of disapprobation, on which succeeding events have built so immoveable a dislike; and I had not known you a month before I felt that you were the last man in the world whom I could ever be prevailed on to marry."

Although Darcy struggled to comprehend such a catalogue of rejection and criticism, yet his convictions of the

soundness of his sentiments as far as her family were concerned gave him some certainty and comfort. Since clearly
there was nothing to be gained by his remaining in the room,
or remonstrating with her further, he said, "You have said
quite enough, madam. I perfectly comprehend your feelings,
and have now only to be ashamed of what my own have
been. Forgive me for having taken up so much of your time,
and accept my best wishes for your health and happiness."

With these words Darcy hastily left the room, opened the
front door and quit the house.

17

When a man has been accustomed since his earliest years to command what he desires, a disappointment in matters nearest to his heart must come as more than a severe shock.

On his return to Rosings, Darcy went upstairs directly, unable to compose his mind enough to spend the evening in the company of his aunt and cousins. He paced his room for half an hour, fury, resentment and dismay within him in equal measure.

He had no qualms about what he had said to Miss Bennet concerning the manners and origins of her family. When she had had time for reflection, she must readily acknowledge them to be true from her own observation. As to her sister's affections, that was—perhaps—a matter on which she might have better information than himself.

It was on the subject of Wickham that Darcy's resentment burned most strongly. What a misfortune for fate to allow that gentleman to poison her mind! He recalled only too well his conversation with her during the dance at the Netherfield ball. Clearly Miss Bennet had been easily deceived by Wickham's narration of his dealings with the Darcy family, and by his pleasing style of address.

At least that deception could be remedied, and she must be trusted with the unhappy story of his sister's encounter with Wickham the previous year. He had confidence in her discretion as to Georgiana's unfortunate entanglement.

Darcy tossed and turned through all the dark hours, composing in his mind a letter that might remove her admiration for Wickham and at least absolve himself from unreasonable prejudices as far as Miss Jane Bennet was concerned.

Eventually, after many hours, Darcy finally fell into a restless sleep. When he awoke, he rose quickly, anxious to complete the task ahead.

Thus it was after a very disturbed night that Darcy sat down in the morning to write.

> *Rosings, eight o'clock in the morning.*
>   *"Be not alarmed, Madam, on receiving this letter, by the apprehension of its containing any repetition of those sentiments, or renewal of those offers, which were last night so disgusting to you.*

Darcy paused, acutely aware of the pain in her dislike of him. Whatever he had in the past anticipated when he should reach the situation of offering for the hand of a woman of status worthy to be his wife, he had never contemplated rejection of his suit.

Nor had he ever thought that he should be told in such

terms of the unwelcome nature of his offer, nor of the manner in which he had made it.

Certainly, he had no regrets about what he had said to Miss Bennet, but his affection for the lady was strong enough for Darcy to wish her to continue reading further into the letter. He picked up his pen again and, dipping it into the inkwell, went on,

> *I write without any intention of paining you, or humbling myself, by dwelling on wishes, which, for the happiness of both, cannot be too soon forgotten, and the effort which the formation, and the perusal of this letter must occasion, should have been spared, had not my character required it to be written and read.*

Again he paused in thought, for her words came too readily to his mind,

> "I might as well enquire why with so evident a design of offending me and insulting me, you chose to tell me that you liked me against your will, against your reason, and even against your character. I have every reason in the world to think ill of you."

Was that the character by which he wished to be known, which he displayed to the world? Darcy shied away from the thought, and wrote on.

> *You must, therefore, pardon the freedom with which I demand your attention, your feelings, I know, will bestow it unwillingly, but I demand it of your justice.*

Two offences of a very different nature, and by no means of equal magnitude, you last night laid to my charge.

The first mentioned was, that, regardless of the sentiments of either, I had detached Mr. Bingley from your sister, and the other, that I had, in defiance of various claims, in defiance of honour and humanity, ruined the immediate prosperity, and blasted the prospects of Mr. Wickham.

Wilfully and wantonly to have thrown off the companion of my youth, the acknowledged favourite of my father, a young man who had scarcely any other dependence than on our patronage, and who had been brought up to expect its exertion, would be a depravity, to which the separation of two young persons, whose affection could be the growth of only a few weeks, could bear no comparison.

But from the severity of that blame which was last night so liberally bestowed, respecting each circumstance. I shall hope to be in future secured, when the following account of my actions and their motives has been read.

If, in the explanation of them which is due to myself, I am under the necessity of relating feelings which may be offensive to your's. I can only say that I am sorry. The necessity must be obeyed and further apology would be absurd.

Again Darcy stopped the flow of his pen, and stabbed it into the ink with such force that he broke the end of the quill. By the time he was ready to continue with another, he had had too much time to recollect his unhappiness, and the pain he felt about what Miss Bennet had said last night.

How, for instance, had she known that he had influenced Bingley against returning to Hertfordshire and to Netherfield? He had confided in no-one about his part in that as far as he could recall, unless . . . He remembered suddenly his conversation with Fitzwilliam on the journey down to Rosings. It was just possible that his cousin had recounted Darcy's care for his friend, and that Miss Elizabeth Bennet had realised that the lady concerned must have been her elder sister.

In any case, his reasons for separating Bingley from Miss Jane Bennet had been sound and well founded. So he continued writing.

I had not been long in Hertfordshire before I saw, in common with others, that Bingley preferred your eldest sister to any other young woman in the country. But it was not till the evening of the dance at Netherfield that I had any apprehension of his feeling a serious attachment.

I had often seen him in love before. At that ball, while I had the honour of dancing with you . . . ,

Darcy paused at this point, with happier memories of that evening, when at last Elizabeth Bennet had agreed to dance with him, the touch of her hand, the way she had turned across the dance until . . . He shook himself, and continued,

. . . I was first made acquainted, by Sir William Lucas's accidental information, that Bingley's attentions to your sister had given rise to a general expectation of their marriage. He spoke of it as a certain event, of which the time alone could be undecided.

From that moment I observed my friend's behaviour attentively; and I could then perceive that his partiality for Miss Bennet was beyond what I had ever witnessed in him.

Your sister I also watched. Her look and manners were open, cheerful and engaging as ever, but without any symptom of peculiar regard, and I remained convinced from the evening's scrutiny, that though she received his attentions with pleasure, she did not invite them by any participation of sentiment.

If you have not been mistaken here, I must have been in error. Your superior knowledge of your sister must make the latter probable. If it be so, if I have been misled by such error, to inflict pain on her, your resentment has not been unreasonable.

Darcy at this point rested his head on his hand, and was deep in thought for several minutes. If Fitzwilliam had told Miss Elizabeth of Darcy's part in the matter, he could not risk discussing her with his cousin, since they knew each other too well for Darcy to be able fully to conceal his feelings from Fitzwilliam. As it was, his cousin had been curious as to why Darcy had been so keen to prolong his stay at Rosings, when he was normally only too glad to get away.

And if Miss Elizabeth Bennet was correct about her sister's feelings, were there other occasions when his own judgement might have been at fault?

For a moment he hesitated. But Darcy was not accustomed to thinking himself in error, and his indignation and confidence reasserted themselves,

But I shall not scruple to assert, that the serenity of your sister's countenance and air was such, as might have given the most acute observer, a conviction that, however amiable her temper, her heart was not likely to be easily touched.

That I was desirous of believing her indifferent is certain, but I will venture to say that my investigations and decisions are not usually influenced by my hopes or fears. I did not believe her to be indifferent because I wished it, I believed it on impartial conviction, as truly as I wished it in reason.

My objections to the marriage were not merely those, which I last night acknowledged to have required the utmost force of passion to put aside, in my own case; the want of connection could not be so great an evil to my friend as to me.

But there were other causes of repugnance, causes which, though still existing, and existing to an equal degree in both instances, I had myself endeavoured to forget, because they were not immediately before me. These causes must be stated, though briefly.

Here Darcy stopped again, for what he must now say was certainly most unlikely to commend his cause to Elizabeth Bennet. However, surely she must realise that such matters could not be overlooked?

The situation of your mother's family, though objectionable, was nothing in comparison of that total want of propriety so frequently, so almost uniformly betrayed by herself, by your three younger sisters, and occasionally even by your father.

Darcy stopped writing, and looked unseeingly out of the window. Her words came back to him

"had you behaved in a more gentleman-like manner . . ."

He shook his head as he continued—

Pardon me. It pains me to offend you. But amidst your concern for the defects of your nearest relations, and your displeasure at this representation of them, let it give you consolation to consider that, to have conducted yourselves so as to avoid any share of the like censure, is praise no less generally bestowed on you and your eldest sister, than it is honourable to the sense and disposition of both.

I will only say farther, that from what passed that evening, my opinion of all parties was confirmed, and every inducement heightened, which could have led me before, to preserve my friend from what I esteemed a most unhappy connection. He left Netherfield for London, on the day following, as you, I am certain, remember, with the design of soon returning.

The part which I acted, is now to be explained. His sisters' uneasiness had been equally excited with my own, our coincidence of feeling was soon discovered; and, alike sensible that no time was to be lost in detaching their brother, we shortly resolved on joining him directly in London.

We accordingly went and there I readily engaged in the office of pointing out to my friend, the certain evils of such a choice. I describe, and enforced them earnestly. But, however this remonstrance might have staggered or delayed his determination, I do not suppose that it would ultimately have prevented the marriage, had it not been seconded by the assurance which I hesitated not in giving, of your sister's indifference.

He had before believed her to return his affection with sincere, if not with equal regard. But Bingley has great natural modesty, with a stronger dependence on my judgement than on his own. To convince him, therefore, that he had deceived himself, was no very difficult point. To persuade him against returning into Hertfordshire, when that conviction had been given, was scarcely the work of a moment. I cannot blame myself for having done thus much.

There is but one part of my conduct in the whole affair, on which I do not reflect with satisfaction, it is that I condescended to adopt the measures of art so far as to conceal from him your sister's being in town. I knew it myself, as it was known to Miss Bingley, but her brother is even yet ignorant of it. That they might have met without ill consequence, is perhaps probable, but his regard did not appear to me enough extinguished for him to see her without some danger.

Perhaps this concealment, this disguise, was beneath me. It is done, however, and it was done for the best. On this subject I have nothing more to say, no other apology to offer. If I have wounded your sister's feelings, it was unknowingly done, and though the motives which governed me may to you very naturally appear insufficient, I have not yet learnt to condemn them.

With respect to that other, more weighty accusation, of having injured Mr. Wickham, I can only refute it by laying before you the whole of his connection with my family. Of what he has particularly accused me I am

*ignorant, but of the truth of what I shall relate, I can
summon more than one witness of undoubted veracity.*

Darcy then went on to relate the whole unhappy story of
his sister's visit to Ramsgate the previous year, of the close attentions that had led her to believe herself in love, and of
Wickham being rapidly despatched from the town when
Darcy had learnt of his designs on Georgiana and her fortune.

*This, madam, is a faithful narrative of every event in
which we have been concerned together; and if you do not
absolutely reject it as false, you will, I hope, acquit me
henceforth of cruelty towards Mr. Wickham.*

For a few minutes, Darcy rested back in his chair, uncertain how best to continue, for he knew not what false stories,
what devious little compliments, Mr. Wickham had paid to
Elizabeth Bennet. He recalled too well what Caroline Bingley had said about them both at the Netherfield ball.

Nor did he know what degree of affection Miss Bennet
still had for Wickham, though Darcy feared that it might,
from her impassioned speech last night, be considerable.

"You have reduced him to his present state of
poverty, comparative poverty. You have withheld the
advantages, which you must know to have been designed for him. You have deprived the best years of his
life, of that independence which was no less his due
than his desert. You have done all this! and yet you
can treat the mention of his misfortunes with contempt
and ridicule."

Darcy sat for a long time in the chair without moving. At length, he roused himself, and took up his pen again.

I know not in what manner, under what form of falsehood he has imposed on you, but his success is not perhaps to be wondered at. Ignorant as you previously were of every thing concerning either, detection could not be in your power, and suspicion certainly not in your inclination.

You may possibly wonder why all this was not told you last night. But I was not then master enough of myself to know what could or ought to be revealed.

Darcy then considered by what other means he could convince Miss Bennet of the truth of what he wrote. He then recalled that she and his cousin Fitzwilliam had been on very good terms during the past days at Rosings, with his easy manners seeming often to commend themselves to her more readily than Darcy's own attentions. That was an unhappy prospect, but at least he could put it to good use.

For the truth of every thing here related, I can appeal more particularly to the testimony of Colonel Fitzwilliam, who from our near relationship and constant intimacy, and still more as one of the executors of my father's will, has been unavoidably acquainted with every particular of these transactions.

Then he added, more painfully,

If your abhorrence of me should make my assertions valueless, you cannot be prevented by the same cause

*from confiding in my cousin, and that there may be the
possibility of consulting him, I shall endeavour to find
some opportunity of putting this letter in your hands in
the course of the morning.*

It was, as he now looked at his watch, a long time since
he had begun to write. There were so many other things that
he could add, that he doubted whether life without her offered him any pleasure at all, that he had hoped to recreate
the happiness that had existed between his own parents in
his union with her, that he had more wealth and position
than any other suitor would be likely to offer her?

But what was the use of writing any of that, after the sentiments that she had expressed the previous day? If he was
to have a chance of passing the letter to Miss Bennet before
luncheon, he must end it now, but how?

At last he wrote, as he felt,

*I will only add, God bless you.
Fitzwilliam Darcy.*

With that, he sealed the envelope, and called his man to
get his clothes quickly, or he feared that he might be too late.

A few minutes later, he left the house, and walked
quickly towards the copse in the park where he had often
encountered Miss Bennet during his stay at Rosings.

The weather had continued fine but, after half an hour
walking back and forth, he feared that his efforts to see her
might be in vain. If she does not come, he resolved, I must
go to the parsonage to leave the letter for her there. He was

about to do this when, turning back alongside the boundary of the park, he caught sight of her by the gate towards the turnpike.

As soon as she saw him, she halted, and went to turn away.

Before she could do so, he stepped forward, and put the letter into her hand, saying, "I have been walking in the grove for some time in the hope of meeting you. Will you do me the honour of reading that letter?" He paused only to take one last long look as she took the paper, and then quickly walked away.

On his return to the house, Darcy was joined by Fitzwilliam. They had agreed previously to go that day to bid farewell to Mr. and Mrs. Collins and their guests. On their arrival at the parsonage, Fitzwilliam decided to wait on discovering that Miss Bennet was not at home. Darcy, however, paid his respects to Mrs. Collins, made his excuses and returned immediately to Rosings.

The last evening there was tedious to both Darcy and his cousin. Fitzwilliam's efforts to promote conversation crossed with Lady Catherine's determination to extract a promise from Darcy to return for another stay within a few months.

Since she did not omit to mention that the prime purpose of her invitation was for Darcy to become better acquainted with his cousin Anne, it was not a suggestion to which he was likely to accede in his current state of mind.

Whatever Miss Bennet had said to him the previous day, she was incomparably more dear to him; and any thought of an alliance to his pale, dull, cousin was unthinkable.

Eventually, in the face of his aunt's persistence, Darcy reverted to his customary silence, leaving Fitzwilliam to carry on some conversation with Lady Catherine as best he could, and take the credit for their stay in Kent having been nearly twice as long as they had originally planned.

It was with no pleasure that Darcy heard his aunt say that she would be making a visit to town in early June, and he had to speak with unaccustomed lack of certainty as to where he might be at that time.

Lady Catherine then advised him that she was also thinking of making one of her regular visits to Bath, in the hope of some benefit to Anne's health from taking the waters. She suggested that Darcy might choose to meet them there. He had eventually to remember a pressing need to write a letter to his steward in Derbyshire about estate business, to escape her persistence about this plan.

The following morning, Darcy took breakfast with Lady Catherine, resisting her every attempt to engage him in any further conversation about his intentions for travelling during the next few months. Happily, she took his silence as indicating his melancholy at leaving Rosings and its occupants, and pressed her conversation on Fitzwilliam instead.

Two hours later, the two cousins had said farewell to their aunt and cousin, and were on the road to London.

Part Four

I declare that I do not know a more aweful object than Darcy, on particular occasions and in particular places.

18

On their arrival in town, Georgiana greeted Darcy and Fitzwilliam.

After enquiring about Lady Catherine and the health of her cousin Anne, Georgiana was soon in conversation with Fitzwilliam about their plans to visit his elder brother in Essex, where a new addition to his family had recently arrived.

"Your sister is getting to be like all ladies—too happy to talk about babies and small children all day if you give them the chance!" said Fitzwilliam cheerfully. "It is just as well that I shall be able to escape to the park with my brother from time to time."

"You are unkind," said Georgiana, smiling at Darcy, "for I am sure that the baby's mother would be very distressed if I did not take an interest. And in any case, I can be useful in helping to keep the elder little boy occupied. Otherwise, that task might fall to cousin Fitzwilliam!"

Fitzwilliam did not seem too worried by this possibility, but Darcy was amused by the exchange, and reflected that, at least amongst people she knew well, his sister was becoming much more confident about taking her part in conversation. To date, her shyness had perhaps appeared to some who did not know her well as indifference, or pride.

That rapidly brought him to the thought that the same could be said about himself, and to the conversation he had in the drawing room at Rosings with Miss Bennet and Fitzwilliam.

What had he said then —

"We neither of us perform to strangers."

That certainly applied to himself; but to her?

His mind wandered on to Miss Bennet's rejection of his suit, and her words then.

> "I might as well enquire why with so evident a design of offending and insulting me, you chose to tell me that you liked me against your will, against your reason, and even against your character? Was not this some excuse for incivility, if I was uncivil?"

That had been a hard thrust for a man to accept who had always prided himself on his propriety of address.

> "You are mistaken, Mr. Darcy, if you suppose that the mode of your declaration affected me in any other way, than as it spared me the concern which I might have felt in refusing you, had you behaved in a more gentleman-like manner."

> "From the very beginning, from the first moment I

may almost say, of my acquaintance with you, your manners impressing me with the fullest belief of your arrogance, your conceit, and your selfish disdain of the feelings of others . . . I had not known you a month before I felt that you were the last man in the world whom I could ever be prevailed on to marry."

"You could not have made me the offer of your hand in any possible way that would have tempted me to accept it."

Oh, what painful recollections these were.

"Darcy! You are not listening to a word I am saying!" cried his cousin.

Darcy came to with a start.

"I beg your pardon," he replied. "What did you want me to do?"

Fitzwilliam looked at him quizzically before repeating,

"Georgiana would enjoy a drive in the park tomorrow before luncheon, now that she has a choice of escort. Which of us is to go with her in the curricle?"

"You should go, for I shall have other opportunities to talk to her another day, when you must be elsewhere," said Darcy.

After this, he was aware during the meal that Fitzwilliam was observing him closely, and he endeavoured to make pleasant conversation to both his companions. They were, after all, the people in the world most dear to him.

Or, at least, had been until he had met a lady with very fine eyes and a lively manner who . . .

Darcy took a grip on himself again, and succeeded in concentrating his attention on Georgiana and Fitzwilliam for the rest of the day.

❊   ❊   ❊

On the following morning, when his sister and their cousin had gone for their drive in the park, Darcy went into the library.

Sitting down at his desk, he closed his eyes. A conversation at Netherfield came to his mind, with Miss Elizabeth Bennet present. What had Bingley said?

"I declare—I do not know a more aweful object than Darcy, on particular occasions and in particular places; at his own house especially, and of a Sunday evening when he has nothing to do."

He had not cared for the remarks then, and had been glad that Miss Bennet had not laughed at him.

But now, except for the time of day, they seemed all too accurate. It appeared that in company he was likely to betray his preoccupation with recent events to those who knew him well and, when alone, he was condemned to relive those same events, moment by moment.

What had he said to Miss Elizabeth in the drawing room at Netherfield?

"My temper would perhaps be called resentful. My good opinion once lost is lost for ever."

But what of hers?

This was a wretched state of affairs. Darcy was not used to reviewing his own conduct critically, and certainly not with any possibility of taking a different view of himself from before.

His thoughts wandered to what the effect of his letter might have been. Even if Elizabeth Bennet was no longer deceived about the character of Mr. Wickham, even if she accepted his opinion of the unsuitability of her connections, of the conduct of her mother, had the manner of his address been so offensive? He wished that he could know what she was thinking, where she was at that moment, anything that might make him feel more at ease with himself.

She was to be in Kent for one more week, he knew, and then was to join her sister Jane in town for a few days before they travelled home to Hertfordshire.

But that knowledge could avail him nothing. He must learn not to care where or how she was.

∾ 19 ∾

These and many other unhappy thoughts continued to trouble Darcy over the days and weeks that followed.

His anxiety to justify what he had said to Elizabeth Bennet, to maintain to himself the correctness of his approach, did not long survive. He soon began to examine and re-examine every part of what he had said, every manner of expression he had used, on that fateful evening in Kent.

There seemed to be no escape from his uneasiness and confusion, which troubled him at every time of day, and wherever he was.

Avoiding as he often did the social round in town, and unable to visit Bingley's house in the country, Darcy was tempted many times to leave for Pemberley and the peace of Derbyshire.

But Georgiana was busy with her music masters in London, and he had not the heart to deprive her of his company without any real excuse, until she went to visit his cousin's family in

Essex. It was some comfort to be with his sister, who was so dear to him. In any case, it seemed very doubtful whether he would gain any more peace of mind by leaving town.

On several occasions, when he was lost in thought, he caught Georgiana looking at him carefully, but she said nothing. Finally, one evening when they were alone, his sister asked him hesitantly, "Is there anything particular troubling you at the moment? I should so like to be of use if there is. You are always thinking of me, and I should like to help you in return."

She coloured as she spoke, as though he might reprimand her, or speak in rebuff.

Darcy was not sure for a moment how best to reply.

For many years an only child, he had been accustomed to being without a confidant where the affairs of the heart were concerned. Until now, Georgiana had always been very much his younger sister, someone for him to protect rather than to share his problems with.

"I am not sure how to answer you," he said slowly. "It is a matter of . . . affection, about someone to whom I would have given no attention previously. Although I do not find our aunt Lady Catherine easy company, I have always shared her view that it is of primary importance to marry well, to seek an alliance with someone of our own consequence. Do you not agree?"

He was surprised to see that she looked very shaken.

Then she said, "Are you referring to Mr. Wickham? To what happened last year, before I had the benefit of your advice?"

"No, no, of course not," he said quickly, anxious to reassure her.

"You were sadly misled, and in any case you had, to begin with, no one, no mother, no one, to turn to."

His sister looked very relieved. Darcy went on, finding himself more comfortable than he had expected in being able to speak to someone about his agony of mind.

"No, I will be honest with you, I am thinking of my own situation. Georgiana, you do understand how important social position and family matters are to me?"

"Too much reliance on that does not often seem to lead to happiness," Georgiana said, reflectively. "I would hope that you would marry someone you find congenial. You do not often seem to find people you admire in town, nor when you went to Hertfordshire, from what you said to me before. Is that not so? And even those people whom you seem to prefer can be very," she paused, "sharp, like Miss Bingley and Mrs. Hurst."

Darcy looked at her in surprise, for his sister had not ventured this opinion to him previously with such clarity.

It was perhaps because he had begun to share her view about Bingley's sisters, after their comments on Miss Elizabeth Bennet in Hertfordshire, that he decided to tell her something of the truth.

"Perhaps you can help me, for I am very troubled in my mind. Whilst I was at Rosings with cousin Fitzwilliam, I met again a lady, a Miss Elizabeth Bennet, whose family come from Hertfordshire, near the house that Charles Bingley took on lease last Michaelmas.

"I realised then that I . . . liked her very much better than many people I have met. Miss Bennet is one of the few people I could rely on to . . . to keep a secret of mine. But her family are not superior, particularly her mother, her mother's family and her younger sisters.

"I met her again because she was visiting her close friend Charlotte Lucas, who has married the rector at Hunsford." Darcy stopped, for he could not bring himself to go as far as saying that he himself had then proposed marriage.

Then he went on, "I spoke to her more . . . plainly . . . than I now think that I should have done, about the importance of connections and social position in marriage. And there were other things on which we disagreed."

"I know that you would like her. She is not only lovely, and amiable, but she is also lively, accomplished in singing and dancing, and plays the piano-forte with pleasure. In truth, I like her very well indeed."

"But how important are her connections, and how can I commend myself to her, in the unlikely event that we should ever meet again?"

The way in which he spoke, with more feeling than she had ever heard him, confirmed to Georgiana that her brother must have said many things that he now regretted.

Georgiana replied slowly, "I am not at all experienced in the ways of the world, as you are. But it seems to me that people are of good breeding if they behave in a genteel manner, are thoughtful and considerate, and not because of who they are, or because they are always proud of how much money or consequence they possess."

She went on, "I know that you and I are well provided for, so surely we do not have to seek a fortune as cousin Fitzwilliam says that he must. I know that he may be jesting, at least a little, but you have this house, and Pemberley, and a great estate, and . . ."

Her courage then began to fail Georgiana, and her voice trailed away, as she began to think that she had said too much.

Her brother had turned and was deep in thought for some minutes.

Then he looked back at her and said, "I believe that you are right. Manners are important, but only if they are genuine. How I wish that I had talked with you before, for I may have said and done things that I may never be able to change, and shall always regret."

Georgiana paused for a moment in case he said anything further.

When he did not, she said softly, "You can not be sure of that. Perhaps the best guide is to treat people, everyone you meet, with the politeness and consideration with which you would wish them to treat you?"

He looked at her in surprise, for this was indeed a novel thought for him.

He could not stop himself saying "Everyone?"

She did not reply, but looked at him steadily.

Darcy then said, "I understand you, but I fear that it may be too late. I do wish that you had been able to meet her."

And with that, he left the room, leaving his sister to wonder what she could do to ease his evident distress.

The subject was not discussed between them any further, but Darcy tried no longer to justify to himself the manner in which he had spoken to Miss Bennet in Kent.

What at the time had seemed to be his proper concern at the inferiority of her connections, the degradation which an alliance with her family would bring, his satisfaction that the concerns he had expressed were natural and just, now seemed hollow, a convenience, to conceal his own insecurity, and feelings of inadequacy in company.

His confidence in the reasons that had led him to separate Bingley from her sister likewise came to diminish, to be an echo of his desire not to measure people by their real worth, to take comfort in social position rather than in genuine character and goodness.

Miss Elizabeth Bennet's words to him on that afternoon at Hunsford came back so often to torture him.

"... *your arrogance, your conceit, and your selfish disdain for the feelings of others* ..."

It was a measure of how much Darcy's view of himself had altered that he now questioned how he would have felt if she had used similar sentiments in speaking to him?

Darcy began to realise that, even if everything he had said to Miss Bennet had been well founded, the way he had expressed himself must have alienated her.

He feared now that his letter, which at the time he had thought had been composed calmly and in order to rectify her errors of knowledge, could only have increased the unfortunate effect of his words. He had thought that he had been rational and measured. Now his recollection was of his dreadful bitterness of spirit at rejection, when he had been so certain of success, of his desire then to demonstrate his superior position in society, and use her family circumstances and connections to denigrate her further.

Thus Darcy tortured himself over many days.

Worst of all was the knowledge that Wickham's regiment was still stationed at Meryton. Elizabeth Bennet was likely to have every chance to be subject to his insidious charms and persuasions.

Although, in more rational moments, Darcy doubted

whether his childhood companion would ever consider marriage to someone who could bring with her as little fortune as Elizabeth Bennet, that gave him no ease compared to the daily opportunities he imagined Wickham having to touch her heart and reinforce the feelings of, at the very least, compassion that she clearly felt for him. He could only hope that she gave some recognition to the intelligence about "that gentleman" as he had set out in his letter.

Georgiana, he knew, found him uncommunicative and distracted and, for her sake, he endeavoured to appear more cheerful than he felt.

When he was with his sister, he succeeded in putting Elizabeth Bennet out of his mind for much of the time. But elsewhere, and particularly through the long sleepless nights, she was never far from his thoughts.

He often had in his mind what Miss Bennet had said to Fitzwilliam at Rosings,

> "Shall we ask your cousin . . . shall we ask him why a
> man of sense and education, and who has lived in the
> world, is ill qualified to recommend himself to strangers?"

And he recalled Fitzwilliam's reply,

> "It is because he will not give himself the trouble."

How much he would give now to have the opportunity to take all the trouble in the world, if it would gain him the affections of Miss Elizabeth Bennet.

20

In due time, his sister travelled with Fitzwilliam to see their cousin, the Earl's elder son, and his young family in Essex, leaving Darcy in town to await the arrival of Bingley and his sisters. One afternoon soon after, when Darcy was just returned from visiting his attorney, an unexpected visitor called, carrying a message from Lady Catherine. It was Mrs. Collins, who explained that she was in town to execute some commissions for herself and for his aunt.

She told him that Lady Catherine had recently travelled to Bath in the hope of bringing some improvement in the health of her daughter by taking the waters at the Cross Bath. His aunt had written to Mrs. Collins to say that their arrival to stay off Laura Place had, as was only right and proper, been included prominently in the list of new visitors for that week in the Bath Chronicle. Anne's condition would not permit them to attend a gathering in the Assembly Rooms, but they had been to a concert in the Pump Room. They had walked in the Sydney Gardens, where they had seen the canal recently built as part of the link between the rivers Kennet and Avon, and they hoped to be able to make an excursion in their carriage into the country round about the city.

Rather than take her daughter home thereafter, his aunt was planning to visit town for a few days before travelling on to Rosings, and had asked Mrs. Collins to tell her nephew of her intention. Darcy was surprised to learn of this, as Lady Catherine usually considered that the polluting air and exposure to too much society in London were injurious to Anne's health. He recollected suddenly his aunt's comments just before he had left Rosings, and asked his visitor whether she knew of any reason why his cousin would be making such a rare visit to town.

Mrs. Collins, looking rather embarrassed, said something had been mentioned, only in passing of course, about the possibility of a marriage for Anne. He did not reply directly, but changed the subject, to talk for a time of the commissions that she had to carry out in town.

He dared not ask after the one person he wished to hear of by name directly, but said "Do you have good news of your friends in Meryton?"

Mrs. Collins acknowledged that she had.

"Mr. Collins is not with you?" he tried next.

"No, Sir, his duties would not permit that. However, before she left for Bath, Lady Catherine had most graciously said that, since I agreed to carry this letter for you, I might use the second chaise as far as the turnpike."

Darcy said that he was glad of that, as some recompense for her trouble.

Hoping to prompt her to some recollection of Miss Elizabeth Bennet, he went on to recall the last time they had met in Hertfordshire, at her father's house, and then at the ball at Netherfield. Happily for him, this had the desired effect.

"Yes, Sir, I recall us speaking together at the ball, and your dancing with my friend Elizabeth. She has such a facility for that pastime."

After a pause, she added more thoughtfully, "I myself have few opportunities now to dance in Kent. But I acknowledge that there are many other consolations."

Darcy recalled what a young lady of his acquaintance from Hertfordshire had said about the marriage between Mr. Collins and the former Miss Charlotte Lucas,

> "his friends may well rejoice in his having met with one of the very few sensible women who would have accepted him, or have made him happy if they had. My friend has an excellent understanding though I am not certain that I consider her marrying Mr. Collins as the wisest thing she ever did. She seems perfectly happy, however, and in a prudential light, it is certainly a very good match for her."

Darcy again thanked her for her trouble in calling, and asked his coachman to take Mrs. Collins to Bond Street, where she could purchase some of the commissions for his aunt.

When she had gone, he reflected that, in his present state of mind, he could not think of anyone he wished to see less than Lady Catherine, and the more so if she wished to pursue her plans for an alliance with his cousin Anne. But he needed an excuse to be absent from London for a few days.

Thus it was that he surprised both his sister and his cousin Fitzwilliam in finding a sudden delight in joining them and renewing his acquaintance with the landscape in Essex, as well as in congratulating his cousin the Viscount and his young wife personally on the recent addition to their family.

By the time Darcy was back in town, a week in advance of his sister, Lady Catherine had travelled on to Kent, leaving behind her a note that left little doubt of her displeasure at not seeing him during her stay in London.

Bingley now also returned to stay in town.

It did not take Darcy long to realise that his friend was still not in the best of spirits. Although he dare not ask him why, it was not difficult to guess. He knew full well that Bingley's separation from Miss Jane Bennet might be the cause of his distress.

He had much more sympathy with Bingley on this occasion than previously, when his friend had bestowed his affections on other young ladies. There can, Darcy admitted to himself, be no better way of appreciating the sufferings of those whose hearts have really been touched by love than having the same affliction yourself.

The arrival of Bingley's sisters at Grosvenor Street with Mr. Hurst two days later did little to cheer Darcy.

He was already regretting the invitation that he had extended to them earlier in the year to join his party at Pemberley for a few weeks. He had little patience now for Miss Bingley's pretensions and, as far as possible, he avoided seeing both sisters, encouraging Bingley to visit them at Mr. Hurst's house. However, he could not now go back on his invitation. At least they would only be at Pemberley for a few weeks before travelling on to Scarborough.

He was suddenly wild to get back to Derbyshire and the familiar pleasures there. However, since Georgiana was to travel with him, he had to wait a few more days before she returned from Essex and they could set off with Bingley, his sisters and Mr. Hurst.

On the second day of their journey, the party reached the town where he and Georgiana usually stayed overnight, and which was only a few hours' journey from Pemberley. The Hursts' carriage had been troublesome, with one of the wheels being far from secure, and it was agreed that it would be better for the carriage to take the last part of the journey very slowly.

He knew that there would be business to attend to at Pemberley with his steward. At the Inn, there was an urgent message sent by the post waiting for him.

Accordingly, Darcy decided to ride on alone with his groom the next day, leaving his sister to travel with Bingley and Mrs. Annesley in his own chaise, and the rest of the party with Mr. Hurst.

"You may need," said Darcy to his friend the following morning before he left, "to go more slowly and stay another night on the way, if that will enable the other carriage to reach my estate without further mishap."

21

A few hours later, Darcy rode across the fields and entered the park around Pemberley.

He turned his mount towards the valley leading down the side of the woods, where he knew that he would catch his first sight of the house.

It was one of his favourite rides within the grounds, with the trees as a backcloth to the vista across the lake. Now, in July, the green of the woods was at its best against the colour of the sky.

In those few days at Rosings when he had hoped to bring Elizabeth Bennet to Derbyshire as his bride, he had dreamt of them walking together across that same grass. How briefly that happy reverie had lasted. How much pain and distress had tortured him since April.

Darcy rode down the slope, along the drive and into the stable yard at the back of the house. The stableboy looked surprised as his master came into view, and explained why he had arrived in advance of the rest of the party. Leaving his horse to be unsaddled, Darcy walked slowly through the arch into the garden at the side, and went to turn towards the house.

As he came out into the sunlight from the shade of the buildings, he saw a lady walking slowly towards him. There was something familiar about the figure . . .

Then he stopped suddenly, immobile, totally startled.

There in front of him, and from her expression equally surprised, was Miss Elizabeth Bennet.

They were within twenty yards of each other, and their eyes instantly met, the cheeks of each being overspread with the deepest blush.

To begin with, Darcy could not move, could not speak, he was so taken by surprise. Then he forced himself to recover sufficiently to draw closer. Walking forward until he was a few feet from her, he tried to speak calmly as he enquired about her health, and then that of her family.

Before he began, she took a step as though to move away but, as he addressed her, she turned back and answered him.

In contrast to their last meeting in the parsonage at Hunsford, Miss Bennet hardly looked at him, and her replies to Darcy's pleasantries were as confused as were his questions to her. Despite his state of mind, he was aware that his enquiries, as to the time of her having left Longbourn, and about her stay in Derbyshire, were so frequent and put in so hurried a manner, as must plainly speak the distraction of his thoughts.

As he spoke, he was conscious of his gardener close by. He was also aware, although less clearly, of a lady and gentleman of fashion a short distance back, as though they might be in company with Miss Bennet.

Eventually, every idea failed him and, after standing a few moments without saying a word, he finally recollected himself. Very conscious that his manner of speaking had none of its usual sedateness, Darcy took his leave of her, bowed, and walked swiftly away.

By the time that he had entered the house, Darcy's agitation of mind had resolved on only two matters.

First, Miss Elizabeth Bennet was at that moment still within the grounds of Pemberley.

Second, his overwhelming desire was to encounter her again before she left.

As he took the stairs towards his dressing room at a rapid pace, he sent one of his servants to see how far the visitors had gone in walking towards their carriage.

When he had changed from his travel stained clothes a few minutes later, the message had come back that the carriage awaited them still, as the gentleman accompanying the young lady had told the coachman that they were to take the walk by the side of the water. Darcy's gardener had been asked to act as their guide along the way.

That route led further along the stream towards a fine reach of the woods and onto some of the higher grounds. There, the opening of the trees gave charming views of the valley and the hills opposite with the woods enclosing both sides of the stream. If they had taken the circuit around the lake, that would bring the visitors after some time in a descent back towards the house, past the edge of the water.

Darcy almost ran from the house and took the route in the opposite direction from that the visitors had taken. After a few minutes, he came to the steep walk amidst the rough coppicewood in one of its narrowest parts beyond a bridge.

At this point, the twists and turns of the path revealed from time to time the path further along the stream. He walked swiftly on.

Eventually, at one of these glimpses of the route ahead, he caught sight of Miss Bennet and her companions coming slowly along that part of the path towards him. He slowed his pace a little and, as they came nearer, Darcy tried hard to compose himself.

Uppermost in his mind were Miss Bennet's comments at their last meeting in Kent about his behaviour. He remembered so well what she had said:

> "your arrogance, your conceit, and your selfish disdain of the feelings of others . . ."

He was only too well aware that he might only have this one opportunity to redeem himself in her eyes. He had long since ceased to deceive himself that any other course would secure his own happiness.

When they met, he greeted her with all the civility he could muster.

She responded in equal politeness by beginning to admire the beauty of the place, saying how delightful and charming it was. He was puzzled that she then stopped speaking abruptly, as though in confusion. In this pause, he asked her if she would do him the honour of introducing her two companions, who were standing a little behind her.

He was not quite sure of her expression. She almost smiled, and then said that they were her uncle and aunt, Mr. and Mrs. Gardiner, from Cheapside in London.

Darcy had taken them for people of fashion. But he was

quick to greet them. With Miss Bennet and her aunt in front, Darcy turned to walk back towards the way he had come.

He soon found in conversation with Mr. Gardiner that he was a cultivated and intelligent man with pleasant manners and a wide range of interests. He expressed a lively curiosity about country pursuits and, for someone who lived in the city, was unexpectedly well informed about them.

The conversation turning to fishing, Darcy invited Mr. Gardiner to fish there as often as he chose, while he continued in the neighbourhood, and offered to supply him with tackle. As they passed alongside the water, he asked the gardener to point out those parts of the stream where there was usually most sport.

After some time, they reached a part of the path close to the brink of the river, and drew close to the water to inspect a plant. At this moment, Mrs. Gardiner sought her husband's arm, confessing some fatigue from the exercise of the morning.

Darcy was secretly delighted by this alteration, since it enabled him to take his place by her niece, and they walked on ahead of the others together.

After a short silence, she spoke, wishing him to know that she had been assured of his absence before she came to the place.

"I understand that your arrival had been very unexpected," she said quickly, "for your housekeeper informed us that you would certainly not be here till to-morrow; and indeed, before we left Bakewell, we understood that you were not immediately expected in the country."

"You are quite right," he said, half turning to steal a

glance at her as he spoke, "for business with my steward had occasioned me coming forward a few hours before the rest of the party."

"They will join me early tomorrow," he continued, "and among them are some who will claim an acquaintance with you. They are Mr. Bingley and his sisters."

Miss Bennet answered only by a slight bow.

At that moment, Darcy knew that he himself coloured, his mind instantly driven back to when Bingley's name had been last mentioned between them. He dared not look, but surmised that hers might be similarly engaged. They walked on a little in silence, their minds thus occupied. Darcy was anxiously considering whether she might agree to an application from him concerning Georgiana.

"There is also one other person in the party," he continued after this pause, "who more particularly wishes to be known to you. Will you allow me, . . . or do I ask too much . . . to introduce my sister to your acquaintance during your stay at Lambton?"

She replied to this with what appeared to him to be pleasure, if not ease, and he engaged to bring Georgiana to the inn at Lambton where they were staying as soon as he could, after his sister's arrival at Pemberley.

They then walked on in silence, soon outstripping the slower pace of her uncle and aunt. When they reached the carriage at the side of the house, Mr. and Mrs. Gardiner were some way behind.

After another pause, Darcy ventured to ask Miss Bennet whether she would take some refreshment inside the house, for he most dearly wished to show her some aspects that might commend Pemberley to her.

However, she declared herself not tired, and preferring to admire the view.

Again there was silence between them, and so many subjects that he thought to pursue were linked with unhappy memories from the past. At last, Miss Bennet began, rather tentatively, to talk of travelling. Her uncle's need to return soon to his business had required them to reduce the extent of their journey, which had been intended to take them to the Lakes. But they had seen Blenheim and Chatsworth, as well as Matlock and Dove Dale.

Her aunt, who had lived some years ago in Lambton, had wished to revisit the village, and had then suggested that they should visit Pemberley.

Miss Bennet again repeated that their understanding had been that the family was not at home, or they would not have planned to call at the house. He in turn expressed his pleasure at having the opportunity of renewing their acquaintance, and of meeting her uncle and aunt. This conversation occupied the time well enough until Mr. and Mrs. Gardiner came across the lawn to join them.

Darcy again pressed his visitors to go into the house and take some refreshment; but this was declined, although with the greatest civility.

He then handed the ladies into the carriage and, as it drove off, walked slowly towards the house.

On his way across the hall, he encountered the housekeeper, Mrs. Reynolds.

"I understand that you have had visitors to see Pemberley today?" he said.

"Yes, Sir. I would not have admitted them if I had known that you were to be at home. But I understood from the young lady that you had met her before. Her aunt told me that she had heard much of you from her niece."

This was welcome news to Darcy. For Elizabeth Bennet to have spoken of himself, and to have seen something of Pemberley, was what he had wanted to hear.

"There is nothing to regret; indeed, I am very glad that they were able to see the house. The young lady lives near Netherfield, the place that Mr. Bingley took last Michaelmas, in Hertfordshire. As they are staying at Lambton, they may be able to visit us again, once Miss Georgiana has arrived tomorrow."

22

In the past, Darcy had prided himself in being able to compose his mind in any situation, if only by avoiding those occasions which could disturb him.

It was as well that he had urgent business to discuss with his steward, for otherwise he would have found himself making very little use of the rest of that day.

In particular, he needed to decide how he could detach Georgiana from Bingley's sisters as soon as might be, so that he could introduce his sister to Miss Bennet.

How much he now wished that he had heeded Georgiana's reluctance to invite the ladies and Mr. Hurst to accompany Bingley to Derbyshire, even though that had been his practice in the past.

The sooner he could introduce Georgiana to Miss Bennet, the more opportunity he would have to see her during the remainder of her stay in Lambton. He so dearly wished to see her again at Pemberley. How he longed to know

whether she might have seen some improvement and soften-
ing in his speech and conversation, and an absence of that
arrogance, and ability to offend and insult, which she had
discerned previously in Kent.

When Darcy recalled his severity in addressing the
habits of her family, what irony there now was in discovering the intelligence, manners and good humour of those very
relatives from Cheapside that Miss Bingley had ridiculed
last winter at Netherfield.

Despite the distractions which he found to occupy him,
the rest of the day seemed to take so long to pass, and the
night the more so, that on the morrow, it seemed impossible
that less than a few hours had elapsed since his sudden encounter with Miss Bennet.

However, he was in a very much more cheerful frame of
mind than he had been for several months. It should be possible during Miss Bennet's stay at Lambton for them to meet
on more than one occasion.

Darcy had left Georgiana to travel with Bingley and
Mrs. Annesley, with Mr. and Mrs. Hurst and Caroline Bingley to follow in Mr. Hurst's equipage.

It was therefore with some surprise that he saw only his
own chaise make its way up the drive towards the house in
good time the following morning.

It transpired that the Hursts' carriage had been delayed
by another problem with one of the wheel bearings. The
innkeeper at the town where they had spent the night hoped
it could be repaired within half a day.

Darcy's other guests were therefore likely to be coming
some hours later.

He wasted no time in taking advantage of this unexpected opportunity. When Bingley went to his room to change soon after their arrival, he went to seek out his sister. He found her examining with delight the new piano-forte that he had purchased, as a surprise present for her arrival at Pemberley.

"Georgiana, I have most welcome news. Miss Elizabeth Bennet, the young lady we last spoke of in town, is staying at Lambton with her uncle and aunt. I have said that we will call on them together, once you arrived. Would you be willing to go with me today, once you have had a late breakfast? I should prefer that, rather than wait until tomorrow."

His sister very readily agreed to this plan, and Darcy then went in search of his friend.

"So you see, Bingley," he ended in explaining the news about the unexpected visitors from Hertfordshire, "I shall have ample time to make the journey to Lambton with Georgiana and then return before your sisters arrive with Mr. Hurst. Will you excuse us both for a short while?"

"Why, yes, if you insist," said his friend, "but I would prefer to accompany you, if I may. I should be very happy to see Miss Elizabeth again. It is so long since we last met in Hertfordshire."

This was not the reply that Darcy had expected, and he deliberated briefly as to what Miss Bennet's reaction to seeing Bingley might be. He was, after all, the man whom she thought had been too easily persuaded to forget her elder sister.

However, it might be a benefit to the good impression that Darcy sought to create in the lady's mind for his friend to be eager to see her. Thus it was settled that Bingley should accompany Georgiana and her brother, and they were soon together in the chaise and travelling across the park towards the Lambton gate.

On their arrival at the Inn, Bingley waited below, and Darcy and his sister were taken into the parlour to see the visitors.

Mr. and Mrs. Gardiner were as affable and pleasant as they had been the previous day. Miss Bennet was much quieter than he recalled when they had met in Rosings, but he was glad to see the trouble she took to make conversation with his sister, who shyly endeavoured to play her role. Darcy wondered if the visitor was thinking of the contrast between Georgiana's unassuming and gentle manner and what she had thought of his own in Kent.

Darcy asked if his friend might join them, and was glad to see nothing but pleasure in Miss Elizabeth Bennet's expression as Bingley came in. He greeted her warmly, and was quickly introduced to her uncle and aunt. Bingley was soon making conversation with them as if he had known them from a much longer acquaintance. How Darcy envied his facility in light conversation. Again, he regretted his own greater difficulty in such matters.

Bingley enquired in a friendly, though general way, after the Bennet family. Darcy did note that, once, his friend asked particularly whether all Miss Bennet's sisters were at home, and the tone of his voice was such that it denoted rather more than just pleasant interest on that point.

He heard his friend then say, "It was a very long time since I have had the pleasure of seeing you," and, before Miss Bennet could reply, he added, "It is above eight months. We have not met since the 26th of November, when we were all dancing together at Netherfield."

She acknowledged this warmly, and Darcy thought that he caught her looking at himself for a moment as she did so.

After some prompting from her brother, Georgiana extended an invitation to the travellers from Hertfordshire to dine with them at Pemberley on the following day. There was a short hesitation, which to Darcy seemed awkward, and perhaps to presage an excuse for refusal, before the answer came. However, Mrs. Gardiner, having glanced at her niece, said that they would all be delighted to accept. Bingley then expressed great pleasure in the certainty of having the opportunity to see Miss Elizabeth again.

Before Darcy and his party left, the invitation to Mr. Gardiner to fish at Pemberley with the gentlemen was renewed, and an arrangement made for the following morning. Miss Bennet looked at Darcy as this was decided, and smiled, as though to thank him.

Thus it was that he returned to Pemberley in a better humour than when he had left, and found no difficulty in being civil to the Hursts when they arrived late in the afternoon. Even Caroline Bingley's obvious distaste for the news of their forthcoming dinner engagement could not harm his contentment.

As he retired for the night, Darcy hoped at least that he had begun to show Miss Bennet that he had lost some of the self-consequence, and unbending reserve which she had so deplored in Kent. If that were the case, then he now needed to be able to reinforce that better impression.

23

The following morning, Mr. Gardiner kept his engagement to fish at Pemberley before noon.

Darcy and Mr. Hurst were there to meet him, together with the other gentlemen of the party. It was some half an hour before a casual remark to his host by Mr. Gardiner alerted Darcy to the fact that Miss Bennet and her aunt were themselves at Pemberley, returning the courtesy of the call made by Georgiana at Lambton the previous morning.

Darcy quickly excused himself and hastened to the house.

There he found the two ladies seated in the saloon, and partaking of some refreshments with Bingley's sisters and Georgiana. Mrs. Annesley was encouraging her mistress to make conversation with Mrs. Gardiner and her niece. Mrs. Hurst and her sister, Darcy noted, were sitting away from the others, and appeared little inclined towards conversation.

Darcy was soon aware that the Bingley sisters watched any move he made to give attention to Miss Elizabeth Bennet.

On seeing her brother, Georgiana came across to greet him, and then went back to sit next to Miss Bennet. Darcy moved to sit near Mrs. Gardiner, who confirmed his favourable impression of the previous day by making conversation with Mrs. Annesley, and including Georgiana in the discourse when there was an opportunity to do so.

Suddenly, Darcy heard Miss Bingley say, with sneering civility,

"Pray, Miss Eliza, are not the ___shire militia removed from Meryton? They must be a great loss to your family."

Darcy turned and looked quickly at her as Miss Bennet replied with apparent calm to this provocation.

Miss Bingley appeared disappointed. At the same time, Darcy noted that she had failed to see that Georgiana had been overcome with confusion at the mention of the name of Wickham.

Her brother then maintained his gaze at Miss Elizabeth Bennet, without seeing that his sister continued to be unable to lift up her eyes.

Darcy was more concerned to see whether Miss Bennet retained any remnant of that interest in Mr. Wickham that had so pained him in Kent.

Her lack of reaction, and her composure despite Miss Bingley's sharp remarks, heartened him. He hoped that might mean that she no longer was deceived by that member of the militia. That thought led Darcy on to reflect that he would never have been prepared to confide in Miss Bingley the information about Georgiana's experience at Ramsgate that he had entrusted to Elizabeth Bennet without any fear of it being revealed.

He soon forgot the mention of that affair in the pleasure of entertaining Miss Bennet under his own roof for the first time. It seemed all too soon before she and her aunt gave their compliments and were escorted by their host to their carriage.

When Darcy returned to the room, Miss Bingley was venting her feelings to Mrs. Hurst in criticisms about Miss Elizabeth's person, behaviour, and dress.

"How very ill Eliza Bennet looks this morning, Mr. Darcy."

He turned to look at her silently, without expression.

"I never in my life saw any one so much altered as she is since the winter. She is grown so brown and coarse! Louisa and I were agreeing that we should not have known her again."

Darcy cared little for this address, but contented himself with coolly replying, that he perceived no other alteration than her being rather tanned, a not surprising consequence of travelling in the summer.

"For my own part," she rejoined, "I must confess that I never could see any beauty in her. Her face is too thin; her complexion has no brilliancy; and her features are not at all handsome. Her nose wants character; there is nothing marked in its lines. Her teeth are tolerable, but not out of the common way; and as for her eyes, which have sometimes been called so fine, I never could perceive anything extraordinary in them. They have a sharp, shrewish look, which I do not like at all; and in her air altogether, there is a self-sufficiency without fashion, which is intolerable."

Darcy, exasperated, allowed himself to appear somewhat nettled at this attack, but again remained silent.

She continued, "I remember, when we first knew her in Hertfordshire, how amazed we all were to find that she was a reputed beauty; I particularly recollect your saying one night, after they had been dining at Netherfield,

"She a beauty! I should as soon call her mother a wit."

"But afterwards she seemed to improve on you, and I believe you thought her rather pretty at one time."

"Yes," replied Darcy, who could contain himself no longer, "but that was only when I first knew her, for it is many months since I have considered her as one of the handsomest women of my acquaintance."

He then left the room to go to his sister, who could be relied upon to take a very different view of Miss Bennet. However, Darcy hoped that his answer would put an end to Miss Bingley's barbed remarks. He had no intention of pandering to her ill feelings.

24

The following day, Darcy could look forward to Miss Bennet and her relations dining at Pemberley.

However, he determined to ride to Lambton that morning in the hope of finding her there. If she would agree to take a turn in the open carriage with Georgiana and himself one afternoon, Darcy could rely on spending a couple of hours in the company of the two people he knew that he now held dearest in all the world.

At the Inn, the servant told Darcy that Mr. and Mrs. Gardiner had gone out, but that Miss Bennet had remained behind, to join them later. Darcy followed him upstairs to the room that he and Georgiana had visited the previous day.

He was met by the sight of Miss Bennet rising from a chair, with a letter in her hand, apparently in a state of great agitation.

Her pallor and manner startled him as he heard her exclaim on seeing him, "I beg your pardon, but I must leave you. I must find Mr. Gardiner this moment, on business that cannot be delayed; I have not an instant to lose."

"Good God! what is the matter?" he said.

Then, recollecting himself, he said "I will not detain you a minute, but let me, or let the servant, go after Mr. and Mrs. Gardiner. You are not well enough; you cannot go yourself."

She hesitated, and then after a moment called back the servant, asking him, in tones of great distress, to fetch his master and mistress home, instantly.

On the servant leaving the room, she sat down, looking miserably ill. Without realising what he did, Darcy took the nearest chair and, leaning forward, took her hand in his.

She seemed unaware of his presence. After a few moments, her apparent distress made him say, very gently,

"Let me call your maid. Is there nothing you could take, to give you present relief? A glass of wine; shall I get you one? You are very ill."

"No, I thank you," she replied, endeavouring to recover herself. "There is nothing the matter with me. I am quite well. I am only distressed by some dreadful news which I have just received from Longbourn."

She then burst into tears, and for a few minutes could not speak another word.

Darcy, in wretched suspense, could only say something indistinctly of his concern, and observe her in compassionate silence. Eventually, she straightened herself in the chair and he reluctantly let go of her hand as she spoke.

"I have just had a letter from Jane, with such dreadful news. It cannot be concealed from any one. My youngest sister has left all her friends and has eloped; has thrown herself into the power of . . . of Mr. Wickham. They are gone off together from Brighton. You know him too well to doubt the rest. She has no money, no connections, nothing that can tempt him to . . . she is lost for ever."

Darcy could find nothing valuable to say.

"When I consider," she added, in a yet more agitated voice, "that I might have prevented it! I, who knew what he was. Had I but explained some part of it, only some part of what I learnt, to my own family! Had his character been known, this could not have happened. But it is all, all too late now."

His first thought on hearing her speak was that she had kept the confidence that he had entrusted to her about Georgiana and Wickham.

The second was that his first thought was unworthy if, by maintaining that silence which he himself had asked, she had been unable to prevent what had now happened to her sister.

Unable to find any words to allay her distress and, as Miss Bennet seemed lost in unhappy thought, he at first kept silent. Then, lest he appeared unconcerned, he said with complete truth, "I am grieved, indeed, grieved and shocked."

Seeking to give her something to hope for, he went on, "But is it certain, absolutely certain?"

"Oh yes! They left Brighton together on Sunday night, and were traced almost to London, but not beyond; they are certainly not gone to Scotland."

"And what has been done, what has been attempted, to recover her?"

"My father is gone to London, and Jane has written to

beg my uncle's immediate assistance, and we shall be off, I hope, in half an hour. But nothing can be done; I know very well that nothing can be done. How is such a man to be worked on? How are they even to be discovered? I have not the smallest hope. It is every way horrible!"

As Darcy shook his head silently, his mind was busy.

Wickham, he recalled, had spent some time during the past few years in London. Indeed, it was there that Darcy believed he had met Mrs. Younge, who had taken charge of Georgiana with such unhappy results. It could be that his sister's unfortunate experience might enable him to trace Wickham when Mr. Bennet and his brother Gardiner could not.

He was roused from his thoughts by Miss Bennet's distressed tones, as she said,

"When my eyes were opened to his real character.—Oh! had I known what I ought, what I dared, to do! But I knew not,—I was afraid of doing too much. Wretched, wretched, mistake!"

Darcy made no answer. That she accepted his opinion of Wickham was so very welcome; his concern now was more for her distress than for the fate that might befall her sister.

However, there seemed to be nothing he could say which might not promise what might not be achievable, or appear facile when he wished to show his genuine anxiety.

At last, and after a pause of several minutes, he felt that he should intrude no longer, and said to her quietly,

"I am afraid you have been long desiring my absence, nor have anything to plead in excuse of my stay, but real, though unavailing, concern. Would to heaven that anything could be either said or done on my part, that might offer consolation to such distress. But I will not torment you with vain wishes, which may seem purposely to ask for your thanks."

Her head was bowed, and she did not reply. After regarding her gravely for some moments, Darcy rose to his feet. Before he turned to leave the room, he suddenly recollected the plans which had been made for them to meet later.

"This unfortunate affair will, I fear, prevent my sister's having the pleasure of seeing you at Pemberley today."

"Oh, yes. Be so kind as to apologize for us to Miss Darcy. Say that urgent business calls us home immediately. Conceal the unhappy truth as long as it is possible. I know it cannot be long."

He readily assured her of his secrecy and concern for her distress, wished for a happier conclusion than might appear likely, and left his compliments for her relations.

As he reached the door, Darcy could not bring himself to leave without turning to give her a last, long, look, for he knew not when he might see her again.

Miss Bennet had lifted her head and, just for a moment, he fancied that there was something in her expression that was more than anxiety; more than regret at his going.

But it was no time to linger, or indulge his own concerns. Without saying any more, he left the room and shut the door behind him.

Part Five

He has been accused of many faults at different times, but this was the true one. Nothing was to be done that he did not do himself.

25

It was in a very different frame of mind from a few hours earlier that Darcy made the journey back to Pemberley.

What changes there had been over the past days and hours to excite his emotions. He had gone from despair, through shock, to pleasure and delight, and back again.

It was some comfort to him that Miss Bennet's aunt and uncle would be travelling with her. They both seemed to be people of a sensible disposition and sound character, on whom she and her father could rely to assist in this unhappy matter.

However, as he rode across the valley towards the house, Darcy was more than ever certain that he should involve himself in the search for Wickham and the youngest Miss Bennet.

He was under no illusion that this intention rested on any regard for either of them. His opinion of the gentleman in particular was incapable of improvement, especially after their encounter at Ramsgate. His dislike had not been lessened by the attraction that might have fleetingly affected Elizabeth Bennet before Darcy had made her aware of Wickham's true character.

At least he had the satisfaction of knowing that deception was over. Indeed, he would be able to think of the lady as *his* Elizabeth in his dreams, now that particular bar to their future acquaintance had been removed.

The recollection of what he had written in his letter at Rosings reminded him forcefully of all that unhappy conversation with her on the evening when he had declared his heart. He thought, ruefully, that his resolution on leaving Rosings to forget his affections and all his memories of the lady and Hertfordshire had come to very little.

His reservations about some of her family had, Darcy feared, been only too justified in respect of her youngest sister. If he now needed to travel at short notice to town, a place which had very little pleasure to offer him in the summer, and to pursue two people for whom he had so little regard, that would be nothing if Elizabeth Bennet might as a result find the situation resolved, and the ill-suited couple brought to marriage.

When he reached the house, Darcy sought out his sister, finding her in the first floor sitting room playing her pianoforte.

"Georgiana, I have to travel to London tomorrow—there is business I have to attend to for a few days."

His sister looked puzzled, for they had only left town some four days earlier.

"It must be very urgent?" she replied.

"Yes," said Darcy, "but I should not be there long."

"Can I not come with you?" said Georgiana.

He looked at her with some surprise, for she usually preferred being in Derbyshire above all else. Since he had observed that Elizabeth Bennet also enjoyed country pursuits, he had wished so much that they could have had more time to become acquainted.

"It is better not. Besides, Bingley and his sisters are here as our guests, and they will be company for you."

He hesitated, and then added, "It would be of help to me if you would entertain them in my absence. I will return directly."

"Mr. Bingley is always very pleasant . . . ," his sister said slowly.

Darcy recalled their conversation in London a few months ago about Caroline Bingley and Mrs. Hurst. "I will ask him to take particular care of you. Do you wish me to speak to Mrs. Annesley also?"

Georgiana replied in the negative.

"Bingley and his sisters are to go on to Scarborough in a couple of weeks' time. If my return from town has to be delayed, I promise that I will let you know directly."

His sister smiled at him. "Thank you. But were not Miss Bennet, her uncle and aunt to join us for dinner tomorrow?"

Darcy had been debating on the journey from Lambton whether to tell his sister about Elizabeth Bennet's urgent return south. It could be concealed without any need to tell a falsehood.

However, he knew that he could rely on his sister to keep a secret.

"Miss Bennet had news from home, so that she must return to Hertfordshire, and is leaving today. It is a private matter, and something that she would not want mentioned abroad. As I must myself be away from here tomorrow, there is no need to tell Bingley or his sisters."

Georgiana looked at him quietly for a moment, and seemed almost to intend a question.

But she only said, "I remember that you once told me in London that Miss Bennet was one of the few people you could rely on to keep a secret of yours. You can be sure that I will not tell the Bingleys, or anyone else. But I shall be very sorry not to see her tomorrow. Shall we meet her again at another time?"

That was a question to which Darcy would dearly have liked to have known the answer himself.

He contented himself with the reply that "Miss Bennet is someone whose acquaintance I value, as you know. I do very much hope that we shall both have the opportunity to see her again."

And with that, Darcy went away to speak to Bingley. His friend, whilst as surprised as Georgiana that business would require him back in town so soon, gladly undertook to take good care of her in his absence. Then Darcy went to his study. He penned a short note to his cousin Fitzwilliam, which was sent immediately to Lambton to catch the express.

The rest of the day was spent pleasantly enough. Miss Bingley and her sister expressed regret that Darcy must leave them on the following morning, but little curiosity and no sorrow that, as a result, Miss Bennet and her relations from the city would not be coming to dine.

Darcy left in his coach at first light the following morning for London.

Without any company to distract him on the journey, his

mind alternated between the events of the past few days and the task that might lie ahead.

What irony of fate was it that Wickham seemed to continue to have the power to injure him in those matters most dear to his heart!

Last year, it had been the attempt to elope with Georgiana from Ramsgate, which had so nearly succeeded. Only a few months ago, he had thought that the first and only person that he had ever wished to marry preferred Wickham to himself and had, as he subsequently discovered, been nearly deceived as to his true character. Certainly, Elizabeth Bennet's opinion of himself had, from her remarks at Hunsford Parsonage, been damaged by Wickham's recital of the history of their acquaintance.

And now, just as a most lucky chance had given him the opportunity to redeem her opinion of him, Wickham had been the reason for Miss Bennet returning to Hertfordshire because of her sister's elopement.

The only remedy must be to find some way of making sure that Wickham married Lydia Bennet, and as soon as possible.

That would doubtless require parting with a significant sum of money. In itself, that concerned Darcy not at all, beyond regret that it should need to be expended on persons for whom he had no regard or respect, and who had no claim on his sympathy or generosity.

There was pain in the thought that he would most probably, if the matter were to be concealed from the world at large, need to locate the fugitives himself and negotiate directly with Wickham in order to achieve a satisfactory outcome to the affair.

At this point, Darcy allowed his mind to stray to Miss Elizabeth Bennet and their recent acquaintance. She had been quiet, so very reserved, compared to their meetings in Kent, that had ended in that most painful encounter when she had rejected his proposal. But earlier, one evening at Rosings, she had conversed with both himself and Fitzwilliam in the lively manner that he had remembered from Hertfordshire.

"Shall we ask him why a man of sense and education, and who has lived in the world, is ill qualified to recommend himself to strangers?"

How such a remark from her with a smile could so touch his heart! He had long come to realise that her lively disposition would be of great advantage in balancing his own tendency to introspection. Her love of the country, her interest in reading, would match his own. And just a little hint of a compliment from Elizabeth Bennet gave him such comfort. And that, he thought, must be sufficient to sustain him until he should ever see her again.

What could the outcome have been if they had only had a little more time together in Derbyshire, perhaps on a drive out into the park at Pemberley? Likewise, the dinner that he had planned would have been another opportunity to try to remove the unfavourable impression she had formed of him.

At least, he might have been able to establish the foundations to take forward their acquaintance. Her uncle and aunt, Mr. and Mrs. Gardiner, had appeared cultivated people with whom he would have been happy to spend more time. With Miss Bennet, they had been most pleasant to Georgiana. He had noted that they had not been overborne by Miss Bingley's manner, and had been courteous to his servants, a habit that lady did not favour. All in all, he was sorry not to have been able to see more of Elizabeth Bennet with her uncle and aunt. Especially in view of his comments to her about her family in April, he would have liked very much for her to have been certain of that.

That thought led him on to speculate about what was at that moment occurring at Longbourn, a house he had never seen. He was sure that Jane Bennet would be grateful for her sister's return home.

Less pleasing were thoughts of the reception that Elizabeth Bennet might get from her mother; the vulgarity and lack of discretion that Mrs. Bennet had displayed so often in company, and on visiting her daughter Jane at Netherfield. Some months ago, the thought of that lady's defects would have been enough for him to think no further of Elizabeth Bennet. Now, they were but an irritation, to be regretted, but ignored.

Thoughts of Netherfield brought his mind to Bingley. His delight in encountering Jane Bennet's sister in Derbyshire had been very evident. If there was to be a successful outcome to the flight of Wickham and the youngest Miss Bennet, then Darcy must address the issue of his friend's affections, which he had himself disrupted. He now tended to accept Miss Elizabeth's judgement of the matter, and therefore that Jane Bennet had reciprocated his friend's affections.

That brought Darcy's thoughts back to his own affections and wishes.

If Elizabeth Bennet was ever to become the wife of a man of consequence and be able to move with ease in his own circle, without any reproach, the union between Lydia Bennet and Wickham must be accomplished. Otherwise, it would be a source of pain and embarrassment that Darcy would not have Elizabeth Bennet bear. At least he had the means, and perhaps Fitzwilliam had the knowledge, to accomplish a satisfactory outcome to that elopement.

What an irony it was that Wickham had pressed his attentions on such different characters as his sister Georgiana and Lydia Bennet, with equal success. Thus Darcy continued as the miles passed, his mind teasing away both at the problem of the moment, and the affections of many months. He might not relish the task ahead, but it must be done.

As night drew on, the coach reached the next town, and he took accommodation for the night.

Darcy left early the following morning and, by late afternoon, he was in his house in town.

He had no intention of contacting Mr. Bennet until some positive outcome seemed likely, so the next day he made various inquiries as to the whereabouts of Wickham and Miss Lydia Bennet, but to no avail. He concluded that he must await the reply to the letter he had addressed to his cousin. That came by the express two days later.

It was brief:

> *Dear Darcy,*
>   *I have received your note, and send my reply by express as you request.*
>   *When I paid Mrs. Younge last year the wages which*

you said should be given to her (which, as you will recall,
I did not agree were due), she had taken a large house in
Edward Street, and was then letting to visitors.

I have had no contact with her since. But I have no
reason to believe that she should have moved from there.

Whatever the reason for you contacting her, I hope
that it has nothing to do with Georgiana.

Yours,
James Fitzwilliam.

Darcy lost no time in calling for his coach, and setting off
for Edward Street.

He located the house in question. Mrs. Younge was at
home, but she was clearly not pleased to see him. Rather, she
was defiant and, to begin with, disclaimed any knowledge of
Wickham or where he was to be found.

It took Darcy several visits over the next two days before
he could get from her what he wanted. It eventually became
clear that she would not reveal where Wickham was without
the assistance of a particular sum of money. But she did
know where he was to be found, and that the youngest Miss
Bennet was with him. Her friend had indeed gone to Mrs.
Younge on his first arrival in London, with the intention of
staying there, but the house was full. So Wickham had gone
to another lodging, only a few streets away.

When he had ascertained what bribe would persuade her
to tell him what he sought, and had passed it over, Darcy obtained the address. He went there straightway, and saw
Wickham. Their conversation informed Darcy that marriage
had never been his design. Wickham told him that he was
obliged to leave the regiment, on account of pressing debts

of honour but, despite Miss Bennet's youth, he had no scruples about laying all the ill-consequences of her flight on her own folly.

After their interview, Darcy insisted on speaking to the lady alone. His first object was to discover whether she would quit her present disgraceful situation, and return to her friends and family, offering his assistance in accomplishing this.

But he found Lydia Bennet resolved on remaining where she was. She cared nothing for the peace of mind of her sisters or any of her family at Longbourn, or for the good opinion of any of her friends. She wanted no help from Darcy and would not entertain the possibility of leaving Wickham. She was sure they should be married some time or other, and it did not seem to much signify when.

Darcy therefore resolved to do what was necessary to secure and expedite a marriage. Wickham had told Darcy that he meant to resign his commission immediately. However, it became clear that he had no firm plans for his future; all he knew was that he should have nothing to live on.

Darcy reminded him that, although Mr. Bennet might not be very rich, he would have been able to do something for him.

"I still hope to achieve a much better fortune elsewhere," Wickham replied. "As you know, I have been unfortunate in my friends and shall not be happily settled without the marriage portion of some wealthy lady to maintain myself."

Darcy did not answer this point directly, but said instead, "I imagine that you will have left behind you debts in both Meryton and Brighton?"

Wickham had to acknowledge that this was so but said

that he was sure that, if he were able to achieve a modest fortune by marriage elsewhere, they could be discharged.

However, persistence on Darcy's part confirmed that, provided that an adequate provision could be made for his debts, that an opportunity should be found for him as an officer in the regulars, and a further amount were to be available to settle on Lydia, Wickham was prepared to contemplate a marriage with the youngest Miss Bennet.

After further meetings, Wickham was persuaded that, although Darcy might have the means to make greater provision for their future, his aversion to at least one of the recipients would not allow him to do more than what was absolutely necessary. At length, Wickham settled for that.

26

The next day was Friday, and Darcy travelled to Gracechurch Street, and left his carriage a short distance away. An inquiry there established that Mr. Gardiner had arrived from Hertfordshire last Sunday, but was not at that moment at home. Mr. Bennet was there, but the servant said that he was to leave early the following morning.

Darcy decided not to leave his name but, after breakfast on the Saturday, he called again hoping to see Mr. Gardiner. He was greeted pleasantly, although with considerable surprise.

Darcy told him that, having some private intelligence not known to others, he had determined to travel to town from Derbyshire. This information had enabled him to find out where Wickham and Lydia were staying.

He went on, "My motive has been that it is my own fault that Wickham's worthlessness had not been so well known, as to make it impossible for any young woman of character, to love or confide in him. My mistaken pride prevented me from laying my private actions open to the world. It is therefore my duty now to endeavour to remedy the evil I have myself brought on."

Mr. Gardiner appeared to be surprised at this, but did not intervene, so Darcy continued. "I had been some days in town, before I was able to discover them."

And he went on to explain the course of his discussions with Wickham, and that matters might be concluded if Mr. Gardiner was willing to agree to them. Wickham's debts in Meryton and in Brighton were to be paid, amounting to considerably more than a thousand pounds, another thousand in addition to her own settled upon Lydia, and his commission purchased in the regulars. The discussion continued for several hours.

They met again on Sunday, Mr. Gardiner seeking this time to persuade Darcy that the cost of the arrangements should fall only on him. But Darcy was adamant that he would bear the expense, with the credit to go to Mr. Gardiner despite his wishes to the contrary.

Finally it was agreed that the attorney should be called upon the following day to draft the necessary papers. At the end of their discussion, Mr. Gardiner told Darcy that Mrs. Gardiner had returned from Longbourn with their children. He had no secrets from his wife, and could rely on her discretion. He therefore would like Darcy to tell her what had transpired. He indicated his agreement, and his host took Darcy into the drawing room.

There, Mrs. Gardiner was sitting with their two little girls, aged about eight and six years.

"My dear," said Mr. Gardiner, "here is a pleasant surprise! Mr. Darcy has come to assist us in this wretched business about Lydia. He will tell you about it."

And Darcy related the progress of his search and his discussions with Wickham.

Mrs. Gardiner's discourse and deportment endorsed Darcy's impression of her as an amiable, intelligent woman. Indeed, the discussion confirmed Darcy's opinion that both the Gardiners were as pleasant as he had found them in Derbyshire only a few days before.

When he had finished his account, Mrs. Gardiner said to him, "Mr. Darcy, we are so very obliged to you for all the trouble you have taken. It would seem best for Lydia to come here for the two weeks until the wedding, especially as her father may not be willing to receive them at Longbourn after the marriage."

And Mrs. Gardiner added, "And may I suggest that the priest at St. Clements may be willing to marry them, as Wickham is living in that parish?"

Darcy told them that he was happy to agree to this plan, and would communicate it to Lydia and Wickham the very next day.

"I will undertake to bring Wickham to the church if the arrangements are made as you suggest. Tomorrow, I will ask my attorney, Stone, to discuss the financial settlement with your man. Did you say that his name is Mr. Haggerston?"

Mr. Gardiner confirmed this. At that moment, the young daughters, who had been playing quietly in a corner of the room, came over to their mother. She smiled at them, and said, "This is Mr. Darcy, who we met in Derbyshire last week with your cousin."

The elder girl, who reminded Darcy a little of Jane Bennet, said to him shyly, "Do you like Elizabeth? She is always very kind and reads so many books to us."

Darcy was conscious that her mother was observing him carefully as he replied, "Miss Elizabeth is a very thoughtful person. She is someone on whom I know I can rely. I too like reading, and hope you do also."

The little girl smiled at him, as her father said to their guest, "Mr. Darcy, we have detained you for a long time on our affairs. Forgive our discourtesy. May we offer you any refreshments?"

"There is no cause for you to apologise, Mr. Gardiner— as I said earlier, this matter is my responsibility rather than yours. I have no particular demands on my time at present. I am on my own in town, and am happy to be of assistance. I must not, however, intrude further into your day of rest. May I call again tomorrow?"

This having been agreed, Darcy went on his way.

27

The following morning, on Monday, Darcy saw Wickham again, and it was arranged that Lydia should go to Gracechurch Street later that day.

Having received their instructions, the two attorneys met, and agreed the principles of the agreements to be drawn up: as soon as that was done, an express was sent off to Mr. Bennet at Longbourn. Darcy took leave of the Gardiners, and promised to be in town again in advance of the wedding in two weeks' time.

He then returned to Derbyshire, to Georgiana and his friends. His short absence did not cause any remark on this occasion, and he told only Georgiana that he would need to return to London for another short stay in due course. She made no comment, although she looked at him thoughtfully. Until he needed to travel again, Darcy exerted himself to be pleasant to Bingley's sisters as well as to his friend, and even to find Mr. Hurst some favourite fishing places to occupy himself. Only in his few opportunities for privacy during the day, and in his room at night, did he allow his thoughts to stray to memories of Elizabeth Bennet and the visit to Pemberley that had given him such pleasure and, for a few days only, such hopes for the future.

When the time came to return to town, he told the assembled company only as they were about to retire the previous night. Bingley was unconcerned, but his sister Caroline appeared to be put out, and remarked sharply to her host, "The Derbyshire air does not seem to agree with you at present, Mr. Darcy!"

Georgiana looked startled at this, and her brother gave her a reassuring smile as he replied to Miss Bingley, "The Derbyshire air agrees with me at any time of year, especially when the company is good. I shall leave Georgiana here again to console you for my absence."

That was not the reply Miss Bingley had been seeking, but she thought it wise not to pursue the matter.

Darcy had considered taking his sister south with him. He could manage to slip away to see Wickham safely married to Lydia Bennet without Georgiana's knowledge, if he had to. However, the possibility that some word might reach her that he had been doing some business with the man who had so cruelly deceived her only the previous year was too great a risk to run.

On Darcy's arrival in London, a letter from Gracechurch Street awaited him. Mr. Gardiner confirmed that Lydia Bennet had been with them since he had left town, and that Wickham had visited her every day. The agreements for the settlement, and for the purchase of Wickham's commission, were ready for signature. Subject to that, Darcy should bring the bridegroom to St. Clements Church at eleven o'clock on Monday.

Mr. Gardiner added that his brother had, as anticipated, at first refused to agree to receive the happy couple at Longbourn. However, another letter from Hertfordshire had recently arrived in Cheapside, to say that the entreaties of his two eldest daughters, Jane and Elizabeth, had persuaded Mr. Bennet to relent. It had therefore been arranged that the newlyweds would leave directly from the church for Longbourn. Mr. Gardiner concluded his note by saying that he and Mrs. Gardiner would be honoured if Mr. Darcy would dine with them in Gracechurch Street on the day after the wedding.

This mention of Elizabeth Bennet's name unsettled Darcy more than he would wish. On several occasions during his discussions with her uncle about Wickham's marriage, Darcy had been tempted to ask after her well-being. Just a little news of how she was would have been sufficient. But he knew full well that he might not be able to maintain his composure at the mention of her name, indeed probably could not. He was close to certain that the Gardiners could be relied upon to be discreet, but he was not willing to risk embarrassing their niece or disclosing his own agony of mind in that respect.

On the Monday morning, Darcy was punctual in his attendance at Wickham's lodgings.

The bridegroom was, as ever, easy in his manners, and in no way disconcerted at the situation that had brought about the need for him to marry a woman for whom, Darcy was certain, he was unlikely to have an abiding affection.

Little was said between them as they were driven to the church. Darcy, however, had some comfort in the thought that it was probably the last occasion when he would ever see his boyhood acquaintance. Whatever the disadvantages of the marriage to the youngest Miss Bennet, the nuptials would at least prevent Wickham seeking any favours from her sister Miss Elizabeth, as Darcy suspected might have happened in the past.

It was therefore with more cheerfulness than might have been expected that Darcy waited beside Wickham.

The bride was delayed, in the event, for ten minutes by her uncle having some final business with his attorney. But by thirty minutes past eleven of the o'clock, the marriage was solemnised, and the new Mrs. Wickham, as unabashed and noisy as Darcy recalled her being at Netherfield, set off with her husband in a chaise for Hertfordshire.

Darcy parted from her uncle and aunt at the church, as he had business to attend to elsewhere in town. His thoughts were often in Hertfordshire during the hours that followed. He could imagine the raptures with which the bride would be met by her mother. How he wished that he could at least see Elizabeth Bennet, to assure himself that the achievement of the marriage might have lifted some of the burden which had fallen upon her at their last meeting in Derbyshire.

Also on his mind was the need to make a decision about Bingley.

He had had the justice to admit to himself that the affection which he had for the second sister could only endorse the right of his friend to have tender feelings for the eldest. More than ever, he regretted that Caroline Bingley and Mrs. Hurst were at that moment at Pemberley. Some way must be found to detach his friend from them, if a visit was to be achieved to Hertfordshire before too long.

In retrospect, for Darcy the most pleasant recollection of his stay in town was dining at Gracechurch Street on the Tuesday.

The family kept a good table and, whilst their home was neither pretentious nor grand, it was furnished with taste, and the company was more than agreeable. From time to time, the names of the two elder nieces were referred to as being regular and valued correspondents with their aunt. Clearly, Mr. and Mrs. Gardiner held both in great affection. The conversation indicated that Jane and Elizabeth Bennet were regular visitors to Gracechurch Street, and the Gardiners and their young family to Longbourn. The names of the other three Bennet sisters, Darcy noted, were little mentioned by comparison.

The Gardiners asked after his sister's health, and gladdened his heart by saying, if only in passing, how pleasant Miss Elizabeth had found Georgiana's company in Derbyshire. That led on to Mrs. Gardiner to comment on the lively and agreeable disposition of her niece, her pleasure in the scenery at Pemberley, and her wish to return in more auspicious circumstances. All this was to Darcy a much happier subject than the idle chatter of Caroline Bingley or Mrs. Hurst, to which he must shortly return.

The following day, Darcy left for Derbyshire, reaching Pemberley late on the Thursday evening.

28

"Mr. Darcy, how we have missed you!" said Miss Bingley, archly, when they met at breakfast the next morning. "Dear Georgiana has been such a gracious hostess to us all, but . . ."

"I am sure," said Bingley quickly, "that none of us could have wished for better, Darcy. I hope that your business in town was concluded successfully on this visit?"

Darcy for once was grateful for his friend's easy manners.

"Yes, thank you."

And he changed the subject quickly, before Miss Bingley or Mrs. Hurst could make further inquiries about what had detained him in London. "Georgiana and I have a plan to take a drive out this morning, as the weather is fine. We can not rely on the rain keeping away for the rest of the week before you leave, so why do we not venture out today while we can?"

Miss Bingley looked disappointed. In view of Darcy's unexpected absence twice in town, she had been hoping for an invitation to extend their stay for a few more days. However, her brother either did not see, or chose to overlook, her less than enthusiastic response to the suggestion, as he warmly endorsed the plan.

By these and other means, Darcy kept the party occupied until the day came for their removal to Scarborough. He maintained in company his normal manner as far as he could, although from time to time his mind was very far away from Derbyshire.

Darcy took the opportunity to have a private word with his friend on the morning when the ladies and Mr. Hurst were busy with last-minute arrangements for the journey.

"Bingley, do you have any plans to return to Netherfield in the next few months? It seems such a long time since we were there. This is a good time of the year to be in that part of the country to shoot for a few weeks."

His friend looked very surprised, as he obviously recalled too well that it had been Darcy, in concert with his sisters, who only last November had persuaded him that he should not visit the house in Hertfordshire again.

"Well, well. No, I had myself not thought of going."

Darcy thought it best to wait for him to continue.

"But," said Bingley after a long pause, "that would be a capital idea. Shall I mention it to Caroline and Louisa now?"

That was not what Darcy had in mind.

In as disinterested a tone as he could muster, he said, "I have no particular reason to suggest it. But if we were to go, it might be better for just a shooting party. There is no need to tell . . . to trouble your sisters about it. After all, they can stay in Scarborough with Mr. Hurst for the next month as they have already planned. You can just join me in town, for a week or more, as you often do."

Darcy paused, to see the effect of these words, and then concluded, "If you then decide that a few days in Hertford-shire would suit you, then no harm would be done. You need not bother your sisters about it."

Bingley, whose brow had been troubled, brightened, and said, "A capital idea! I can settle them in at Scarborough, and then slip away to join you as you suggest."

And on that basis the matter was left.

After Bingley's party had gone, Darcy joined Georgiana in her sitting room. If Bingley were to go south, as now seemed likely, he would have to leave his sister again to go to Hertfordshire.

Georgiana was seated by the window and looked up as he entered the room.

Before he could speak, she surprised him by saying, "You want to return south, do you not? Is it to see Miss Elizabeth Bennet? Is she likely to become someone you . . . more than value? I would happily stay here with Mrs. Annesley, if that was so."

Darcy was taken aback. He had thought that the reason for his confusion of mind had been better concealed over the past few days. He had no certainty in any case that he would, or could, see Elizabeth Bennet at Longbourn. How-ever, his sister's question did give him an opportunity to share his hopes with her, without revealing why he had lately been in town.

"I do not know, Georgiana. I do so wish that I did. But it is a possibility. Would you wish me well in that direction?"

At first she made no reply, but instead came across the room and took his hand. She held it for several moments, and then said, softly, "There is nothing I would like better. But do not worry, I shall keep your secret, whatever happens."

Darcy looked down at her, and for once he had no words to say.

He tried to be patient over the next week. There was much to do on the estate, the library needed his attention, as well as many matters of business. In all such things, and in his sister's company, he tried to take as much pleasure as he did normally. But at the back of his mind, there was the ballroom at Netherfield, a lady dancing gracefully, and a conversation between them.

> "I hear such different accounts of you as puzzle me exceedingly. . . . if I do not take your likeness now, I may never have another opportunity."

A few days later, a letter arrived from Scarborough. Bingley, in confirming that he planned to travel south at the beginning of the next week, inquired whether Darcy would be in town so that he might stay with him.

Darcy sent back a reply in the affirmative.

He stayed a few more days in Derbyshire, and the subject of Miss Elizabeth Bennet was not mentioned between the brother and sister again. Instead, Darcy spent most of his time with Georgiana, and he was able, at least for some of the time, to forget the possible encounters that lay ahead. On the Friday, Darcy bade farewell to his sister, gave her to Mrs. Annesley's charge, and left for town.

Part Six

Where there is a real superiority of mind, pride will always be under good regulation.

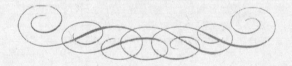

29

When Bingley arrived, he told Darcy that he had already sent word to open up Netherfield House ready to receive them, at least for the next few weeks, and servants were sent on ahead to prepare for the shooting party. By the Wednesday, the two friends were ready to leave town for the journey to Hertfordshire.

As they reached the outskirts of Meryton, Darcy's thoughts were full of the last time he had been there. The chaise passed the assembly rooms where he had disdained to dance with Miss Elizabeth Bennet, past the place in the main street where he had encountered her walking with Mr. Collins and Mr. Wickham. It seemed so long ago, and as though a different person from himself had been there.

Bingley had been quieter than usual on the journey. However, the now familiar landmarks led him to remark on local acquaintances.

Darcy decided that this was the time to broach the possibility of a visit to Longbourn after they had settled in.

"I know that you may wish to shoot as soon as may be. But I would suppose," he said, more casually than was his wont, "that we might encounter the Misses Bennet during our stay here? I have heard that the youngest is now married, to an officer, but her elder sisters may be at home."

"That," said his friend quickly, "would be a capital idea. I have arranged for shooting for the next two days, but perhaps after that . . ."

At dinner, Bingley called back memories of the ball at Netherfield the previous November. By comparison, the house seemed to Darcy to be very empty, although he was far from regretting the absence of Mrs. Hurst and her sister. He was, however, anxious about the reception they might receive at Longbourn, in particular because Miss Elizabeth was aware of his part in separating her sister Jane from Bingley. Whatever her relief at the outcome of her youngest sister's elopement, and her recent knowledge of Wickham's character and behaviour, that might remain between them.

However, his heart would not allow him to forego a visit to the Bennets' house. So, on the third morning after their arrival in Hertfordshire, Bingley and Darcy rode out from Netherfield.

On entering the house at Longbourn, they were met with that unfortunate combination of excessive politeness and vulgarity which Darcy had always found so distasteful in Mrs. Bennet. They found the four eldest daughters together at their work. As he entered the room, Darcy glanced quickly at Miss Elizabeth, who did not seem to lift up her eyes.

Bingley, Darcy noticed, looked both pleased and embarrassed. However, he soon took the chance to make some little conversation with Miss Jane Bennet, who received them both with tolerable ease, and with a propriety of behaviour free from any symptom of resentment.

Darcy was aware that, whilst Bingley had been received by Mrs. Bennet with a degree of civility, this contrasted with the cold and ceremonious politeness of her curtsey and address to himself.

In the face of this, Darcy, after enquiring of Miss Elizabeth how Mr. and Mrs. Gardiner were, said scarcely anything, and Miss Elizabeth was very silent, saying as little to either Darcy or Bingley as civility would allow. But Darcy knew her well enough to observe that she was attending to her work with an eagerness that it did not often command.

As far as he could tell, she had ventured only one glance at himself. He was not seated by her, and so looked around the room. He had often imagined what Longbourn might be like. As he had surmised, it was modestly furnished, but was pleasing by contrast with the grandest and most formal houses he knew, such as Rosings.

As the conversation flowed on, he concentrated on looking more at the eldest sister than at Elizabeth, to see if he could gauge what Miss Bennet's reaction to seeing his friend Bingley again could be.

With her mother so close, he in any case had little opportunity to speak to the daughter with whom he wished most to converse. There could be no possibility in this room of that happy ease they had begun to establish together in Derbyshire, or even the comparative freedom at Rosings when out of the hearing of Lady Catherine. Miss Elizabeth did enquire after Georgiana, but said no more.

"It is a long time, Mr. Bingley, since you went away," said Mrs. Bennet. "I began to be afraid you would never come back again. People say, you meant to quit the place entirely at Michaelmas; but, however, I hope it is not true. A great many changes have happened in the neighbourhood, since you went away. Miss Lucas is married and settled."

She paused briefly for breath, and Darcy took a quick look at the second daughter, at this reference to her friend. He thought that Miss Elizabeth glanced at him at this reminder of the parsonage at Hunsford, but he was not certain. Meanwhile Mrs. Bennet continued unabated.

"And one of my own daughters. I suppose you have heard of it; indeed, you must have seen it in the papers. It was in the *Times* and the *Courier*, I know; though it was not put in as it ought to be. It was only said, 'Lately, George Wickham, Esq. to Miss Lydia Bennet,' without there being a syllable said of her father, or the place where she lived, or anything. It was my brother Gardiner's drawing up too, and I wonder how he came to make such an awkward business of it. Did you see it?"

Bingley replied to Mrs. Bennet that he was aware of the marriage, and made his congratulations.

Darcy reflected with some satisfaction that the mother of the bride should be singularly ill-informed about the matter if her brother had kept his promise. He did, however, look keenly at her second daughter again at this mention of Wickham, and fancied that she met his glance for a moment, before her eyes dropped again to her needlework.

"It is a delightful thing, to be sure, to have a daughter well married," continued the mother, "but at the same time, Mr. Bingley, it is very hard to have her taken such a way from me. They are gone down to Newcastle, a place quite northward, it seems, and there they are to stay, I do not know how long. His regiment is there; for I suppose you have heard of his leaving the ___shire, and of his being gone into the regulars. Thank Heaven! he has some friends, though perhaps not so many as he deserves." And, saying this, she looked pointedly at Darcy.

He noticed that neither of the two elder daughters were looking very comfortable at this mention of their new brother. Mrs. Bennet's outburst drew from Miss Elizabeth a question to Bingley, whether he meant to make any stay in the country at present.

"A few weeks, he believed."

But the mother was not to be gainsaid.

"When you have killed all your own birds, Mr. Bingley," she said, "I beg you will come here, and shoot as many as you please, on Mr. Bennet's manor. I am sure he will be vastly happy to oblige you, and will save all the best of the covies for you."

In observing his friend and Miss Jane Bennet, Darcy had already decided that Bingley found her as handsome as he had last year; as good-natured, and as unaffected.

And she, in as far as he could tell without her sister to assist him, was certainly quietly happy to see his friend again. At least, he told himself, that part of the mission had been accomplished to his own satisfaction so far.

When they rose to go away, Mrs. Bennet invited them to dine at Longbourn in a few days' time.

"You are quite a visit in my debt, Mr. Bingley," she added, "for when you went to town last winter, you promised to take a family dinner with us, as soon as you returned. I have not forgot, you see; and I assure you, I was very much disappointed that you did not come back and keep your engagement."

Bingley looked awkward at this, but said something to the effect that he had been prevented by business. He added that they would be very happy to accept an invitation for the next Tuesday, and so he and Darcy took their leave.

Over the next few days, it was clear to Darcy that his friend was in a much more settled frame of mind. He himself was sad, irritated and far from good company until Tuesday.

He could see no way of repairing or continuing his friendship with Miss Elizabeth with her mother always present. Indeed, he felt that he might be nearly back to the situation and the relationship with her second daughter where he had been after his visit to Kent.

It was therefore with no great anticipation of pleasure that he set off with Bingley to Longbourn as arranged, where there was a large party assembled. When they had repaired to the dining-room, and after a little hesitation, Bingley took the place by Miss Jane Bennet. Darcy was much less happily settled, being seated on one side of Mrs. Bennet, a situation not likely to give pleasure to either, and a considerable distance from her second daughter. They spoke very little during the repast, and there was little enthusiasm for conversation when they did. Darcy had no pleasure either in talking to the young lady on his other side. He took some comfort that Miss Elizabeth Bennet seemed to have even less conversation with the gentlemen sitting to each side of her.

When he finally came into the drawing-room after dinner, the ladies had crowded round the table, where Miss Bennet was making tea. Miss Elizabeth was pouring out the coffee, but the seats near her were already filled. Darcy, who would normally have drunk tea, decided on this occasion to take coffee. However, on his approaching, one of the girls moved closer to Miss Elizabeth, so that he had no option but to take his cup and then walk away to another part of the room.

When the throng had eased, he went to bring back his cup, and was warmed by her saying immediately before they were interrupted again, "Is your sister at Pemberley still?"

"Yes, she will remain there till Christmas."

"And quite alone? Have all her friends left her?"

"Mrs. Annesley is with her. The others, Miss Bingley and the Hursts, have been gone on to Scarborough, these three weeks."

He wished that they might speak more, and so stood by her for some time. But with others so close, and with one young lady whispering to her once more, he had no chance of more conversation and so had to go away again.

When the tea-things were removed, and the card tables placed, the ladies all rose. Before he was aware of what had happened, Darcy was forced against his inclination to join in a game of whist. He and Miss Elizabeth were at different tables, so that he could have no more enjoyment. Their carriage came ahead of the others, so that there could be no reason for he and Bingley to linger.

30

A few days more were passed by shooting on the Nether-field estate and, from his friend's frequent comments and compliments about the lady, Darcy was satisfied of Bingley's serious attachment to Jane Bennet. He took every opportunity to agree with his friend about her charms and happy disposition.

Indeed, Darcy went as far as to add that he had seen over the recent meetings at Longbourn a partiality in the lady for Bingley of which he had not previously been certain, and which his friend confirmed to him was reciprocated.

Darcy then resolved that he must tell his friend that he, as well as Bingley's sisters, had known of Miss Bennet being in London for three months last winter. Darcy had rarely seen Bingley angry, but this was one such occasion. It was clear that this deception wounded his friend greatly.

Darcy made no excuses, thinking it best to admit quite

simply that he had been wrong, and acknowledged the justice of this reaction, saying that his only excuse had been that he had been unaware of Miss Bennet's attachment to Bingley at that time.

On this occasion, as on others, Darcy noted how quickly his friend was prepared to forgive and forget. Unlike myself, Darcy thought. Bingley, unwilling to prolong his disquiet in view of his friend's opinion that Miss Bennet might now receive his addresses with pleasure, soon turned his anger on his sisters. When that also was spent, they agreed that Bingley should go to Longbourn again on the morrow.

"Will you accompany me?"

"No, you must excuse me, for I have had a letter from town, and must be there straightway to attend to some matters of business concerning my estate."

"In any case," Darcy added with a smile, "you will find me an encumbrance if you are really intending to find an opportunity soon to make your addresses to Miss Bennet!"

Bingley acknowledged that this might be the case. He failed to observe that his friend appeared to have received no recent messages from London.

Darcy left that morning, saying that he would probably return to Netherfield in ten days' time.

On the journey to town Darcy reflected, not for the first time, that his friend was very easily deceived.

In truth, there had been no urgent business to take him away, except that he could take the opportunity to express his thanks in person to his cousin, Fitzwilliam, for locating Mrs. Younge, thereby leading Darcy to where Wickham and Lydia Bennet had been living.

Rather, the thought of Bingley's joy at having his ad-dresses accepted, as Darcy was confident would be the case, was not something that he wished to see at first hand. This was particularly so, compared to his own lack of certainty that Miss Elizabeth Bennet had formed any favourable view of himself.

At Longbourn when he had visited there, she had hardly looked him in the eye, and they had had almost no opportu-nity to converse. He had indeed observed her embarrass-ment at the contrast between her mother's mode of address to Bingley and to himself. But that was no different to his recollection of her reaction during Mrs. Bennet's visit to Netherfield last winter, when Jane Bennet had been ill, so it gave him very little comfort.

The future, therefore, seemed bleak, and far less than he had hoped for when he had travelled to Hertfordshire. Whilst he had some comfort in having owned his deception to Bingley as far as Miss Jane Bennet was concerned, his own prospects did not look promising.

He therefore wished to be anywhere but Netherfield when the likely outcome of his friend's intended declaration was confirmed. How he wished that Georgiana was in town rather than at Pemberley. How he would value having her again as his confidant! Darcy could only resolve to keep as busy as he could with his business affairs in town until he heard from Hertfordshire.

What he could not decide in his own mind was his course of action thereafter. Since he had suggested his return to Netherfield, it would seem odd, to say the least, if he did not do so. What other options were there?

❖   ❖   ❖

On arriving at his house in London, Darcy wrote a note to his cousin, Fitzwilliam, who was lodging at the house of his elder brother, Viscount ———, in Brook Street.

A prompt reply arrived, inviting Darcy to take luncheon there on the Wednesday. But before that day came, and four days after leaving Netherfield, Darcy received a letter from Bingley.

Three sides of paper conveyed the happy news that he had finally found an opportunity to convey his affections to Miss Bennet, and that she had accepted him. There then followed a detailed account of the kind reception that Mr. and Mrs. Bennet, not to mention their three other daughters at home, had given to this news.

Bingley went on to give details of the early plans for the wedding, and the need to make various other arrangements. He had heard from his sisters in Scarborough that they would be leaving for the south shortly, so that Darcy might like to call on them before he returned to Hertfordshire.

The letter ended by regretting Darcy's continuing absence, and hoping that his friend might soon rejoin him in Hertfordshire to share in his happiness. A postscript added how the pleasant company of Miss Elizabeth Bennet was consoling his friend when her elder sister was occupied elsewhere.

This news left Darcy with mixed reactions.

He had no intention of making his presence in town known to Miss Bingley and Mrs. Hurst. Their lack of courtesy to Miss Elizabeth Bennet in Derbyshire was still fresh in his mind. Any joy that those ladies might express about their brother's news would be insincere at best, bearing in mind their actions last winter.

Whilst on the one hand he rejoiced in his friend's happiness, he also reflected that the forthcoming marriage of Bingley with the eldest Miss Bennet would inevitably bring him into more frequent contact with her sister.

He could not come to a view of what would be more painful to him; not to see Miss Elizabeth at all, or to encounter her where she might find more pleasure in the company of other eligible gentlemen.

At least he had the comfort, from their last conversation in Lambton, of knowing that she had come to accept the true nature of Mr. Wickham, even if it had since been necessary for that gentleman to become her brother-in-law so that her concerns about her youngest sister should be met.

On the Wednesday, Darcy found Fitzwilliam waiting for him at the house in Brook Street.

"My brother and his family will join us shortly," his cousin said. "How is Georgiana?"

"She is well," Darcy replied, "and has Mrs. Annesley with her at Pemberley."

"Tell me, Darcy, why you wanted to locate Mrs. Younge?" said Fitzwilliam, with a quizzical smile. "I would have thought that she was the last person in the world you would want to meet again after what happened at Ramsgate last year."

Darcy recollected that Fitzwilliam had only just returned from the north, and might be unaware of the marriage between Wickham and the youngest Miss Bennet. However, his cousin was likely to hear the news by some means or other, so there seemed little point in dissembling too much about the matter.

"I wished to be of some assistance in discovering the

whereabouts of George Wickham. He had taken advantage of another young lady, whose parents were anxious to discover her. But, I do not want my part in the matter to be broadcast abroad. So I hope that you are willing that yours also should not be commonly known."

Fitzwilliam regarded his cousin with some amusement. "I have heard that Wickham has recently married the youngest sister of a lady whose company you seemed to enjoy in Kent some months ago. However, I will keep your secret, and have no need to publish my small part in the affair."

Darcy would have welcomed the opportunity to hear his cousin reiterate his good opinion of Miss Elizabeth Bennet. However, he was not anxious to risk revealing his own current agony of mind. So he contented himself with saying, "It is true that he has now married Miss Lydia Bennet. It was a sorry business."

At that moment, they heard voices in the hall, and the Viscount came into the room with his wife and small sons. Darcy was glad of the interruption. The subject was not revisited during the hours that followed, before he took leave of them.

31

Having visited his attorney the following day, Darcy returned to his own house in the afternoon. He was surprised to find a carriage with a familiar livery waiting outside.

On entering, he found his aunt standing in the drawing room. It was immediately clear that she was very angry indeed.

"Darcy," she said imperiously, "I have come here direct from Hertfordshire to see you!"

He, startled, regarded her with a dawning apprehension.

He knew of no acquaintance of hers who might have taken his aunt to that county. He did, however, know some of his own, and one in particular . . .

His worst fears in that regard were soon realised.

"I went to Longbourn this morning, to see Miss Elizabeth Bennet."

Lady Catherine looked at him for some reaction, but seeing none visible then continued, "A report of a most alarming nature had reached me, that not only is the eldest Miss Bennet on the point of being married to your friend, Mr. Bingley, but also that Miss Elizabeth Bennet would, in all likelihood, be soon afterwards united to you, my own nephew!

"Of course, I went to her father's house to insist that she should have such a report universally contradicted."

Lady Catherine paused, and looked at him for agreement. Darcy maintained his composure, and waited for his aunt, for she showed every sign of continuing.

"I was not surprised to find that Mrs. Bennet was in every respect as ill-favoured as I had been led to expect."

Darcy still kept silent.

"I asked Miss Elizabeth whether you had made her an offer of marriage since, as almost your nearest relation, I am of course entitled to know all your dearest concerns.

"She replied that I was not entitled to know hers!"

"I told her that any such match that she had the presumption to aspire to could never take place, since your late mother and I were agreed, when you were both in your cradles, that you and your cousin Anne should be united in marriage. Miss Bennet should know that honour, decorum, prudence, nay, interest, would forbid such a match. She would be censured, slighted, and despised, by every one connected with you.

"She had the impudence to reply that, whilst these would be heavy misfortunes, your wife must have such extraordinary sources of happiness necessarily attached to her situation, that she could, upon the whole, have no cause to repine."

His aunt was totally unaware of the effect that her report of these last few words had on her nephew. The words ran through and through his mind, as Lady Catherine continued.

"I told her that I would not be dissuaded from my purpose by such remarks. I have not been used to submit to any person's whims, or been in the habit of brooking disappointment. I told Miss Bennet that, if she were sensible of her own good, she should not seek to quit the sphere in which she had been brought up."

Lady Catherine looked at Darcy again for his support. He gave none.

"Miss Bennet had the audacity to reply that, in marrying my nephew, she would not consider herself as quitting that sphere; that you are a gentleman; and that she is a gentleman's daughter; so in that you would be equal.

"I made it quite clear that I knew how inferior are the connections of her mother's family. But that appeared to be of no concern to her.

"Instead, she said that, whatever her connections might be, if you did not object to them, they could be nothing to me!

"She did admit to me that she is not engaged to you. I asked her to promise me never to enter into such an engagement."

Darcy concealed his anxiety as best he could, as he waited to hear her next words. It seemed to him a very long moment before she spoke but, when she did, her report was everything that he could have hoped to hear. However, it was clearly contrary to what his aunt had intended.

"She had the effrontery to reply that she would make no promise of the kind."

Darcy let out his breath silently, as his aunt went on, with mounting indignation.

"Indeed, she said that, in any case, her giving such a promise would not make a marriage between you and my dear Anne at all more probable."

He certainly did not dissent from that view, but said nothing as his aunt continued.

"I told her that I am no stranger to the particulars of her youngest sister's infamous elopement. I know it all; that the young man's marrying her was a patched-up business, at the expense of her father and uncles. Such a girl is of course totally unsuitable to be your sister by marriage, as is the son of your late father's steward to be your brother."

Darcy reflected to himself that, if his aunt had really "known it all," her words would have been much more extreme. Her reaction if she had been aware that Darcy himself had brought the whole matter about could only be imagined. He did not remind himself that he might have shared his aunt's views not so many months ago.

"I charged her that she had no regard for your honour and credit, that a connection with her must disgrace you in the eyes of everybody."

"She replied that she was resolved to act in that manner, which would, in her own opinion, constitute her own happiness, without reference to me, or to anyone so wholly unconnected to her."

"When I told her that she appeared to be determined to ruin you in the opinion of all your friends, and make you the contempt of the world,

"She replied that neither duty, nor honour, nor gratitude, had any possible claim on her, and that no principle of either would be violated by her marriage with you."

His aunt paused and, getting no response from him, she then said, with every appearance of expecting a favourable reply, "Darcy, you will appreciate why I was most seriously displeased. *You* must give me the assurances which that ungrateful young woman has withheld."

To reinforce her point, she went on to repeat sentiments that, although less explicitly, she had told him many times before.

"As my nephew, you and Anne are formed for each other. Both of you are descended on the maternal side from the same noble line; and, on the father's, from respectable, honourable, and ancient, though untitled families. You have been destined for each other by the voice of every member of our respective houses. You are not to be divided by the upstart pretensions of a young woman without family, connections, or fortune!"

There was a silence for a few moments and she awaited his reply.

Darcy found himself quite calm, now that the time had come for him to speak. He looked his aunt directly in the eye as he began.

"I have the greatest respect for my cousin Anne, and for you, and that will continue," he said. "However, I would wish to achieve in my own marriage the happiness and affection which my mother and father shared. As to whom I should marry, that is a private matter which I do not intend to discuss with anyone. It is not my wish to offend, but the intervention of others is not calculated to assist me, or to influence my choice."

Lady Catherine regarded him with alarm and dismay, and her voice rose to an angrier pitch as she said, "Are you refusing to give me the assurance I seek? She is a young woman of inferior birth, of no importance in the world, and wholly unallied to the family! Such a marriage would be against the wishes of all your friends! Your alliance would be a disgrace; her name would never even be mentioned by any of us."

She looked again at Darcy for a response, but he remained silent.

"Are you refusing to honour the agreement between your dear mother and myself? Will you not promise me never to enter into such an engagement?"

"My mother told me of no such agreement. I know myself of none. I have no wish to upset you, and I have every respect for my mother's memory," Darcy replied, quietly. "But, as I have already said, there are other considerations to which I give priority."

"I cannot believe," said his aunt, "that you are willing to put aside the wishes of your nearest family in this matter!"

Darcy looked at her without expression, and said nothing.

And although Lady Catherine continued in the same vein for fully fifteen more minutes, he would not yield.

Eventually, his aunt left, in as angry a mood as he had ever seen her, without the assurances that she had sought.

32

Darcy found himself with such a mixture of emotions after Lady Catherine had left that it was some time before he was able to think calmly.

He was at first at a loss to know how the idea of an alliance between himself and Miss Elizabeth Bennet might have occurred to his aunt.

Then he recalled that Mrs. Collins' family lived in Hertfordshire. The news of Bingley's engagement would have travelled to his aunt by that route, and might have prompted speculation about a liaison between himself and the sister of Jane Bennet. It would be also from her chaplain, Mr. Collins, that Lady Catherine would have heard of the recent marriage between Lydia Bennet and Wickham.

His aunt had apparently therefore made a special journey to Hertfordshire, for the sole purpose of obtaining a promise from Elizabeth Bennet which, in her own words only four months ago in Kent, that lady should have been more than happy to give.

Yet she had refused to provide such an assurance.

He could well imagine that Miss Elizabeth might have been more than offended by Lady Catherine's manner of address. Indeed, he had to acknowledge that he and she shared the disadvantage of some close relations who cared little for discreet conversation. However, he did not believe that his aunt's outspoken comments would have prevented Elizabeth from speaking her views plainly.

> "You could not have made me the offer of your
> hand in any possible way that would have tempted me
> to accept it."

He remembered only too painfully those words she had said to him only a few months ago in the parsonage at Hunsford; and others —

> "You are mistaken, Mr. Darcy, if you suppose that
> the mode of your declaration affected me in any other
> way, than as it spared me the concern which I might
> have felt in refusing you."

And, above all,

> "Had you behaved in a more gentleman-like man-
> ner . . ."

How those words had tortured him since then!
What a contrast did Miss Elizabeth's answer to Lady

Catherine now appear, which had just been repeated to him,

> " . . . that his wife must have such extraordinary sources of happiness necessarily attached to her situation, that she could, upon the whole, have no cause to repine?"

Those words touched in him such depths of emotion as he had rarely felt able to admit to himself before.

They indicated a state of mind in the speaker which had seemed to be impossible only a few months ago. He found it difficult to believe that Lady Catherine would have had any reason to fabricate such a remark.

Was it conceivable that Elizabeth Bennet had really said those words? For the first time since she had rejected his addresses in April, he felt some confidence that she might have changed her mind about marriage to him.

Darcy had seen at Rosings that she would have not been in any awe of Lady Catherine. Surely, she would not have hesitated to tell his aunt what she thought, if she had been irrevocably decided against him?

Darcy reflected that he should at least be grateful to Lady Catherine for making the journey to Hertfordshire, if only for the nature of the intelligence which she had brought back with her, and his first thought was to return to Netherfield the very next morning. Then he recollected that he had made arrangements to see his cousins in Brook Street again the next day.

In any case, his agitation of mind was such that it might be more prudent to keep to his original arrangements, and delay his departure.

So Darcy contented himself with sending a note to Bingley, congratulating him on the happy news, and advising that he would be returning to Hertfordshire himself at the end of the week.

The next two days seemed to pass very slowly and, though Darcy reviewed the conversation with his aunt to himself, both by day and during each night, he was no nearer any certainty in knowing what Miss Elizabeth Bennet's true feelings might be.

However, he did resolve that he could not bear much more delay in finding out, and decided that he would accompany Bingley on his first visit to Longbourn once he had reached Hertfordshire.

"Darcy! I am the luckiest of men, and my dear Jane and I have been waiting to share our joy with you!" said his friend when Darcy entered Netherfield.

"I can see," said Darcy, "that you are as happy as I had expected! And are you now a welcome member of the Bennet family?"

"I have been at Longbourn every day since I wrote to you. Their kindness is overwhelming, and Mr. Bennet is being everything affable," said Bingley. "Mrs. Bennet seeks to meet my every need, and my dear Jane's sisters are all attention, especially Elizabeth, as I wrote to you."

"But you will not guess who has been a recent visitor to Longbourn," his friend went on.

Bingley then related the intelligence already known to Darcy, which reminded him of an encounter only a few days ago in town.

"Your aunt Lady Catherine! Apparently she came to see

Elizabeth, for they went off into the copse and had a long conversation together. Jane and I did not know who the visitor was, or I would have greeted her myself, and so we went to talk without interruption in the shrubbery. My new sister must be a great favourite of your aunt's from her visit to Rosings at Easter, to be so favoured!"

It was impossible to compose any answer to this that could be conveyed to Bingley or that Darcy was prepared to reveal. Indeed, his friend's comment was so far from the truth that Darcy decided to change the subject immediately.

"So you and Miss Bennet are to be married before the end of the year?"

"Yes," replied Bingley, "and we shall live at Netherfield, at least to begin with."

Darcy reflected to himself that such an immediate proximity to Mrs. Bennet would not be his own preference, but then his friend was of a less demanding and much more forgiving disposition than himself.

Bingley then went on to enumerate all the many qualities in the eldest Miss Bennet of which he always had been convinced, and of all his expectations of enduring felicity.

Darcy listened to this recital with more patience than he might have found in the past. There was pain indeed in hearing of happiness that he might be unable ever to replicate for himself. But the occasional mention of Miss Elizabeth in his friend's words was of some small comfort to him in his own present uneasiness of mind.

Darcy was about to ask whether the arrangements for the following day included both the elder Miss Bennets when his friend pre-empted him.

"I am going to Longbourn again tomorrow to see Jane.

You must join me, and perhaps we can take a walk with some of her sisters into the countryside round about, if it proves to be a nice day. I know that Elizabeth enjoys the countryside. Indeed, she had told me that she had great pleasure when she was in Kent in walking through the park at Rosings."

This reminder of his most recent visit to Kent brought back so many unhappy memories for Darcy that he thought that they must be visible on his face.

But Bingley continued to talk about his pleasure in his new situation until it was time to retire, and did not appear to notice Darcy's distress.

Part Seven

DARCY: *I can remember some expressions which might justly make you hate me.*

ELIZABETH: *Think only of the past as its remembrance gives you pleasure.*

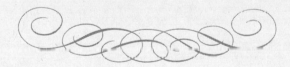

~ 33 ~

After greeting her family the following morning, it was agreed that Bingley and Jane Bennet, and Darcy with the Misses Elizabeth and Catherine Bennet, should take a walk together. To begin with, they went towards the Lucases, because Kitty wished to call upon Maria. With Bingley and the eldest Miss Bennet walking very slowly and lagging behind, Darcy and her sister Elizabeth continued on together. To start with, both were silent.

Darcy was contemplating the best way to start the subject he wished to address when she began to speak:

"Mr. Darcy, I am a very selfish creature; and, for the sake of giving relief to my own feelings, care not how much I may be wounding yours."

Darcy glanced at her in surprise.

Could it be that she had in mind his aunt's recent visit, notable, if the account he had heard was accurate, for Lady Catherine using language that would have given offence to any one? His aunt's remarks had hardly been calculated to improve his companion's opinion of his family.

But she continued, "I can no longer help thanking you for your unexampled kindness to my poor sister. Ever since I have known it, I have been most anxious to acknowledge to you how gratefully I feel it. Were it known to the rest of my family, I should not have merely my own gratitude to express."

Darcy, who had thought that his actions were a secret known only to her uncle and aunt, and to Mr. and Mrs. Wickham, was taken unawares.

"I am sorry, exceedingly sorry," he replied, in a tone of surprise and emotion, "that you have ever been informed of what may, in a mistaken light, have given you uneasiness."

He added, more cautiously, "I did not think Mrs. Gardiner was so little to be trusted."

Her quick reply soon gave him comfort at least as to that.

"You must not blame my aunt. Lydia's thoughtlessness first betrayed to me that you had been concerned in the matter; and, of course, I could not rest till I knew the particulars."

After a few moments, she continued, more slowly.

"Let me thank you again and again, in the name of all my family, for that generous compassion which induced you to take so much trouble . . . and bear so many mortifications . . . for the sake of discovering them."

Darcy immediately recollected the last time they had spoken privately together at Lambton, and the distress that she had confided to him, in the knowledge that he would not betray it. He recalled his decision then to pursue the fugitives, no matter what it cost him, so that she could regain that peace of mind which he believed that only he had the power to restore.

"If you will thank me," he replied, "let it be for yourself alone."

"That the wish of giving happiness to you, might add force to the other inducements which led me on, I shall not attempt to deny."

He chose his next words with care, remembering part of another conversation which they had had at the parsonage at Hunsford in the Spring.

"But your family owe me nothing. Much as I respect them, I believe, I thought only of you."

She was silent and, after a short pause, Darcy then added, "You are too generous to trifle with me. If your feelings are still what they were last April, tell me so at once."

The chasm of pain which this opened up, unhappily so familiar over the past few months, came vividly to his mind, and he had to pause and gather all his resolution before he could continue.

"My affections," he paused, "and wishes are unchanged." He stopped, and then went on, "But one word from you will silence me on this subject for ever."

It seemed to him a very long pause, although in fact it was only a few moments, before his companion began to speak.

"Mr. Darcy, I recollect now with great distress the manner in which I replied to your offer in April. . . . Although I was then certain that I spoke with justice and without prejudice, I have long since come to a completely contrary view. My understanding at that time of Mr. Wickham's situation, and his own and partial account of your role in his affairs, had influenced my mind to an extent which I now consider to have been unpardonable."

She went on quickly, "Although I then felt also that you

were misguided about my sister's feelings for Mr. Bingley, I hope that I also now have the honesty to acknowledge the difficulty for someone not very well acquainted with Jane to have been aware of them."

She paused, and he took a quick glance at her before she continued speaking.

She had uttered the next sentence, and had begun another, before he was able to comprehend the full import of what she was saying.

"As to my own affections, it is some time since I came to realise that, far from maintaining the sentiments that I expressed in April, my future happiness depends on your having a continuing regard and affection for me. Indeed, my feelings are such that I am so very happy to accept your present assurances."

And at last she raised her head, and met his eyes for a moment, before dropping hers again before his gaze.

They walked on, and it was some distance before Darcy had sufficient control of himself to speak.

"I find it difficult to find words which can adequately express my emotions . . . to be confident . . . to know that you return my affections," he began.

"And our separation, since we parted in Derbyshire in July, has only served to confirm how valuable and necessary to me is your regard. That you could ever consent to be my wife has at times seemed to be so impossible that I have been close to total despair. It has been a dream which it seemed could never come true."

He glanced at her as he continued, "And you will have to remind me very often from now on that I am not dreaming!"

He saw her smile at this, although she could not encounter his eye, and he went on to tell her how important she was to him, and for how long he had hoped for this day.

They walked on. There was so much to be thought, and felt, and said.

Darcy recounted his aunt's visit to his house on her return through London, how Lady Catherine had related her journey to Longbourn, its motive, and the substance of her conversation with Elizabeth.

"She thought, by repeating her conversation with you, to obtain that promise from me, which you had refused to give. Some of what she told me," said Darcy, "taught me to hope as I had scarcely ever allowed myself to hope before. One phrase in particular,

> " . . . that my wife must have such extraordinary sources of happiness necessarily attached to her situation, that she could, upon the whole, have no cause to repine?

"Words cannot express how I felt when I first heard her repeat those words, except that at last I had some hope that we might one day find happiness together."

Darcy stole a quick glance at Elizabeth, and thought that her face was luminous with such a smile that . . . but he recollected himself and went on to say,

"I knew enough of your disposition to be certain, that, had you been absolutely, irrevocably, decided against me, you would have acknowledged it to Lady Catherine, frankly and openly."

He saw that Elizabeth coloured and laughed as she replied, "Yes, you know enough of my frankness to believe me capable of that. After abusing you so abominably to your face, I could have no scruple in abusing you to all your relations."

"What did you say of me, that I did not deserve? For, though your accusations were ill-founded, formed on mistaken premises, my behaviour to you at the time, had merited the severest reproof. It was unpardonable. I cannot think of it without abhorrence."

"We will not quarrel for the greater share of blame annexed to that evening," said Elizabeth. "The conduct of neither, if strictly examined, will be irreproachable; but since then, we have both, I hope, improved in civility."

Darcy demurred at that. "I cannot be so easily reconciled to myself. The recollection of what I then said, of my conduct, my manners, my expressions during the whole of it, is now, and has been many months, inexpressibly painful to me."

As his recollection of that evening at Hunsford returned to him, he said,

"Your reproof, so well applied, I shall never forget:

"had you behaved in a more gentleman-like manner.

"Those were your words. You know not, you can scarcely conceive, how they have tortured me. Although it was some time, I confess, before I was reasonable enough to allow their justice."

"I was certainly very far from expecting them to make so strong an impression," said Elizabeth. "I had not the smallest idea of their being ever felt in such a way."

"I can easily believe it. You thought me then devoid of every proper feeling, I am sure you did. The turn of your countenance I shall never forget, as you said that I could not have addressed you in any possible way, that would induce you to accept me."

"Oh! do not repeat what I then said. These recollections will not do at all. I assure you, that I have long been most heartily ashamed of it."

After they had walked on a little, Darcy mentioned the letter he had written after that meeting.

"Did it," said he, "did it soon make you think better of me? Did you, on reading it, give any credit to its contents?"

Her reply confirmed that, although in some respects it had at first angered her, over a longer period of time all her former prejudices against him had been removed.

"I knew," said Darcy, "that what I wrote must give you pain, but it was necessary. I hope you have destroyed the letter. There was one part especially, the opening of it, which I should dread you having the power of reading again. I can remember some expressions, which might justly make you hate me."

"The letter shall certainly be burnt, if you believe it essential to the preservation of my regard," she replied, "but, though we have both reason to think my opinions not entirely unalterable, they are not, I hope, quite so easily changed as that implies."

He thought for a few moments, and then said, "When I wrote that letter, I believed myself perfectly calm and cool, but I am since convinced that it was written in a dreadful bitterness of spirit."

Elizabeth would not let him be so harsh on the author.

"The letter, perhaps, began in bitterness," she replied, "but it did not end so. The adieu is charity itself."

Then she went on firmly, "But think no more of the letter. The feelings of the person who wrote, and the person who received it, are now so widely different from what they were then, that every unpleasant circumstance attending it, ought to be forgotten. You must learn some of my philosophy. Think only of the past as its remembrance gives you pleasure."

"I cannot give you credit for any philosophy of the kind," said Darcy.

"Our retrospections must be so totally void of reproach, that the contentment arising from them, is not of philosophy, but what is much better, of ignorance. But with me, it is not so. Painful recollections will intrude, which cannot, which ought not to be repelled. I have been a selfish being all my life, in practice, though not in principle. As a child I was taught what was right, but I was not taught to correct my temper. I was given good principles, but left to follow them in pride and conceit.

"Unfortunately an only son, for many years an only child, I was spoilt by my parents, who though good themselves, my father particularly, all that was benevolent and amiable, allowed, encouraged, almost taught me to be selfish and overbearing, to care for none beyond my own family circle, to think meanly of all the rest of the world, to wish at least to think meanly of their sense and worth compared with my own.

"Such I was, from eight to eight and twenty; and such I might still have been but for you," turning to her as he said, "dearest, loveliest Elizabeth! What do I not owe you! You taught me a lesson, hard indeed at first, but most advantageous. By you, I was properly humbled. I came to you without a doubt of my reception. You showed me how insufficient were all my pretensions to please a woman worthy of being pleased."

"Had you then persuaded yourself that I should?" she asked him with surprise.

"Indeed I had. What will you think of my vanity? I believed you to be wishing, expecting my addresses."

"My manners must have been in fault, but not intentionally I assure you. I never meant to deceive you, but my spirits might often lead me wrong. How you must have hated me after that evening?"

Darcy stopped walking along the lane, and turned to face her, as he said vehemently,

"Hate you! I was angry perhaps at first, but my anger soon began to take a proper direction."

Elizabeth replied, as if to quell his remorse and direct his thoughts away from what had happened between them in Kent, "I am almost afraid of asking what you thought of me when we met at Pemberley. You blamed me for coming?"

"No, indeed," replied Darcy, "I felt nothing but surprise."

"Your surprise could not be greater than mine in being noticed by you. My conscience told me that I deserved no extraordinary politeness, and I confess that I did not expect to receive more than my due."

"My object then," replied Darcy, "was to show you, by every civility in my power, that I was not so mean as to resent the past; and I hoped to obtain your forgiveness, to lessen your ill opinion, by letting you see that your reproofs had been attended to."

A smile came to his lips as he went on,

"How soon any other wishes introduced themselves I can hardly tell, but I believe in about half an hour after I had seen you."

Darcy then told her of Georgiana's delight in her acquaintance, and of her disappointment at its sudden interruption. Elizabeth looked surprised as he went on to tell her that his intention of travelling to London to find Wickham and her sister had been formed before he had quitted the inn. His gravity and thoughtfulness there had arisen from no other struggles than what such a purpose must comprehend. She expressed her gratitude again, but neither of them wished to dwell on that subject.

After walking several miles in a leisurely manner, and too occupied to know anything of it, they found that it was time to return to Longbourn.

"What could have become of Mr. Bingley and Jane!" she exclaimed, and that brought on a discussion of their affairs.

Darcy said that he was delighted with their engagement, and that his friend had given him the earliest information of it.

"I must ask whether you were surprised?" said Elizabeth.

"Not at all. When I went away, I felt that it would soon happen."

"That is to say, you had given your permission. I guessed as much."

Darcy admitted that it had been pretty much the case, and told her that he had admitted his part in keeping Bingley and Jane Bennet separated when she had been staying with the Gardiners in London during the winter.

"His surprise was great. He had never had the slightest suspicion. I told him, moreover, that I believed myself mistaken in supposing, as I had done, that your sister was indifferent to him; and as I could easily perceive that his attachment to her was unabated, I felt no doubt of their happiness together."

"Did you speak from your own observation," said she, "when you told him that my sister loved him, or merely from my information last spring?"

"From the former," replied Darcy. "I had narrowly observed her during the two visits which I had lately made her here; and I was convinced of her affection."

"And your assurance of it, I suppose, carried immediate conviction to him."

"It did. Bingley is most unaffectedly modest. His diffidence had prevented his depending on his own judgement in so anxious a case, but his reliance on mine, made every thing easy. I was obliged to confess one thing, which for a time, and not unjustly, offended him. I could not allow myself to conceal that your sister had been in town three months last winter, that I had known it, and purposely kept it from him. He was angry. But his anger, I am persuaded, lasted no longer than he remained in any doubt of your sister's sentiments. He has heartily forgiven me now."

Darcy saw Elizabeth smile a little at this but, in contemplating the happiness of Bingley and Jane, which of course was to be inferior only to their own, Darcy continued the conversation till they reached the house.

In the hall they parted.

"My dear Lizzy, where can you have been walking to?" said her elder sister when she entered the room a short distance ahead of Darcy. The rest of the company made the same enquiry as they took the vacant seats at opposite sides of the dining table. Elizabeth replied that they had wandered about till she was beyond her own knowledge but, although she coloured as she spoke, neither that, nor anything else, caused suspicion.

After the meal, the evening passed quietly enough. He observed his friend and the elder Miss Bennet talking together and laughing. Elizabeth was quiet, only giving him an expressive smile when no one else was looking in her direction; but Darcy was more than content with that.

34

On the way back to Netherfield, Darcy told his friend of the day's events.

Bingley was taken totally by surprise.

"Jane and I have talked of that," he began, "but we had concluded that it was impossible."

He went on, "I must say that I had thought, when we met Elizabeth in Derbyshire, at Lambton and Pemberley, that you might have some susceptibility in that direction, despite my sisters' efforts to decry it. But, since then, nothing confirmed to me that you had any such intentions."

Bingley paused and then, as though suddenly struck by a new idea, went on,

"I knew that Lady Catherine had called to see Elizabeth at Longbourn, for Jane told me about the visit. Was that on your behalf?"

"No! It was not," said Darcy, more sharply than he intended.

He reflected immediately to himself that it was not wise, at least not yet, to broadcast his aunt's strong opposition to the marriage, even to as close a friend as Bingley, until he had written to her and received a reply to the letter. There was, after all, the possibility, however small and remote, that Lady Catherine might change her mind about the match.

Instead, he said to Bingley, "Will you now wish *me* joy?"

His friend replied emphatically, "With all my heart. I can think of nothing that would please Jane and I more. Are you to speak to Mr. Bennet tomorrow?"

"Probably, yes," Darcy replied, "when I have had the opportunity for some further private conversation with Elizabeth. Are you willing to propose another walk tomorrow? I must confess that there seems little likelihood of talking with her at Longbourn without being overheard."

"Of course!" said his friend, "for clearly such exercise is to your advantage!"

On the following day, Darcy followed his friend into the drawing-room at Longbourn.

As soon as they entered, Bingley looked at Elizabeth so expressively, and shook her hand with such warmth, as left no doubt of his good information. Soon afterwards, he said aloud, "Mrs. Bennet, have you no more lanes hereabouts in which Lizzy may lose her way again to-day?"

Darcy saw Elizabeth look at him with some alarm, but her mother intervened before she could say anything.

"I advise Mr. Darcy, and Lizzy, and Kitty," said Mrs. Bennet, "to walk to Oakham Mount this morning. It is a nice long walk, and Mr. Darcy has never seen the view."

"It may do very well for the others," replied Mr. Bingley, "but I am sure it will be too much for Kitty. Won't it, Kitty?"

Kitty owned that she had rather stay at home.

Darcy confirmed to Mrs. Bennet that he had a great curiosity to see the view from the Mount. Elizabeth said nothing, but went to get her wrap before joining him outside. After they had walked out of earshot of the house, Darcy began.

"I wish to speak to your father tonight, to ask his consent, before anyone else has any knowledge of it. Do you know what his reaction will be?"

Elizabeth replied, "My father is likely to be very surprised at your application. He knows nothing of what passed between us in Kent, or at Pemberley."

She blushed as she went on, "His opinion of you may be coloured by the views of others, formed when you first came into Hertfordshire."

"You mean, I suppose, by views similar to your own at Rosings?"

She acknowledged that she had in mind something of the sort.

"Also, it is only a few days ago, just after Lady Catherine called, that my father received a letter from Mr. Collins. He wrote that word had reached Kent of my sister's forthcoming marriage. That must have led on to the idea of an alliance between us, passed on, I assume, from Sir William and Lady Lucas to Charlotte, and warned my father that your aunt was opposed to it. He called me into the library, as he was so surprised at such a possibility."

"And what did you say?" said Darcy with a half smile.

"I said as little as I could, without telling him an untruth."

Darcy looked concerned. He knew that Elizabeth was her father's favourite child. "You are not saying that he will refuse me consent to marry you!"

"No, I do not believe so. But he may say that he has had no inkling that I have any attachment to you."

"And your mother, what of her," Darcy inquired, remembering very well Mrs. Bennet triumphantly relating to him only two weeks ago the news of her youngest daughter's nuptials.

Elizabeth told him that she would speak to Mrs. Bennet only when she was certain that Darcy had her father's consent. She went on to ask him, in relation to the events which had led to her sister's marriage with Wickham, what, if anything, should be disclosed.

"As I told you before, Sir, my mother and father have no inkling of how indebted they are to you in that unhappy business. They believe that it was my uncle Gardiner's doing. You do not wish me to inform either of them?"

"Only, if you consider it essential, to tell your father, so that he may not trouble your uncle about repayment."

Elizabeth then reserved to herself passing on the news to Mrs. Bennet, once it was certain that her father had agreed, saying only that she believed that she would always be happy at the prospect of a wedding for any of her daughters. That reminded them both of Wickham and Lydia, and they changed the subject quickly, to happier topics about the future.

35

That evening after dinner, Darcy followed his host when he left the party to go to his room.

Seeing him, Mr. Bennet said, "Can I assist you, Sir? You are very welcome to borrow one of my books, for when the other entertainments, that are on offer, pall?"

"Thank you, but I have no need of a book for that reason. But there is something that I should like to discuss, if you would be kind enough to allow me a few minutes."

Mr. Bennet looked surprised, but said nothing, and he led the way into the library, then inviting his guest to sit down.

But Darcy walked over to the fire, and turned, taking in the room with comfortable furniture and lined with books, in which he knew that his host spent much of his time.

He began, without delay.

"I have an application to ask of you, Sir, that is of the utmost importance to me. Your daughter, Miss Elizabeth, has done me the greatest honour in telling me that she is willing to accept my offer of marriage, subject to your consent."

His host appeared to take several moments to comprehend the import of this request. His countenance turned slowly to astonishment and then to concern. At last, Mr. Bennet said, "You have asked Lizzy to marry you . . . and she has accepted?" He spoke as though expecting a reply in the negative.

Darcy replied simply, "Yes, Sir, she has done me that honour."

"Forgive me, Mr. Darcy," said Mr. Bennet, "but I had no idea that you . . . that she . . . that you and Lizzy were well acquainted enough to . . . ? "

Darcy waited for a moment, and then, as his host made no move to continue, he said,

"Your daughter has told me, Sir, that you may have little knowledge of our meetings in Kent and in Derbyshire earlier this year. You may wish to speak to her about that."

Mr. Bennet was still silent.

"All I should say for myself now is that it is my dearest wish that she should be my wife."

Darcy hesitated for a moment and then, as Mr. Bennet still gave no reply, he added, "I can assure you, Sir, that it is my intention to make a most generous settlement on her in the event of our marriage. She shall not want for anything."

This last remark aroused Mr. Bennet into speech, although not on the lines that Darcy had anticipated.

"I do not doubt your ability to provide for her . . ." he said.

But he went on, in a tone that was almost puzzled, "I had no idea that there was any mutual feeling between you and

my daughter. And I must confess that I was completely unaware of your intentions."

"Forgive me, Sir," said Darcy, "if I say that Miss Elizabeth and I are perhaps less open, more private in our emotions and behaviour than my friend, Bingley, and your eldest
daughter, Miss Bennet."

"Yes, yes," said Mr. Bennet, almost testily, and he then
lapsed into silence.

Darcy was not sure how to interpret this reaction, especially since he had noted in the past that Elizabeth's facility
with words was inherited from her father.

After a pause, he said, hesitantly, "Are you willing to give
me your consent, Sir?"

Mr. Bennet looked at him for a moment, and then said
slowly, "Yes. But, if you agree, I should like to speak with
Lizzy before . . . before the news is passed on to anyone else
in the family."

It was not difficult for Darcy to guess who he had in
mind.

"Of course, Sir. Thank you. I know that Elizabeth . . .
that your daughter greatly values your opinion." And with
that, Darcy went out of the library, and returned to the
drawing-room.

His absence did not seem to have been noted, except by
Elizabeth, since most of the others were busily engaged
playing cards. He smiled at her when he was sure that the
others were occupied and, after a few minutes when he
could do so without being noticed, he approached the table
where she was sitting with Kitty.

While pretending to admire her work, Darcy said in a
whisper, "Go to your father, he wants you in the library."

❀   ❀   ❀

His anxiety in her absence was hard to bear, and it seemed to him a very long delay before she returned.

After so many difficulties over the past few months, he was far from complacent that her father would agree to the match without demur. There might well yet be some objection that he might put to his favourite daughter, which could carry some weight with Elizabeth.

At last, when the evening was almost over, and it was close to the time that he and Bingley must go back to Netherfield, she returned to the room and resumed her seat. When the time came for them to leave, Mrs. Bennet and the rest of the family were busy with Bingley and Jane, and Darcy took the opportunity to speak to Elizabeth.

"Your father . . . ," he began, sounding more anxious than he had intended, and finding that he could not go on.

Elizabeth answered the unspoken question for him. "He is willing to accept my assurances," she said simply, and then suddenly smiled so happily that Darcy nearly forgot the others in the room standing close to him.

For once, he was grateful for Mrs. Bennet's intervention.

"Mr. Bingley is waiting for you in the coach, Mr. Darcy," she said sharply, and he took his leave.

36

After saying goodnight to Bingley, Darcy went to his room at Netherfield, but found himself disinclined to sleep.

The events of the past two days had given him little time for reflection.

Although not of a disposition which relied on the approbation of others, he wished at that moment that he had someone to whom he could confide his joy in the happy future which now lay before him.

Bingley was a good friend, but he was not someone to whom Darcy had ever displayed his innermost feelings, and his cousin Fitzwilliam was elsewhere. Then he recalled his conversation with his sister when they were last together.

She had been so much more perceptive than he had expected when she had asked him,

"You need to return south, do you not? Is it to see Miss Elizabeth Bennet? Is she likely to become someone you . . . more than value?"

He had paused, before deciding to answer her honestly.

"That is already the case, in truth. But as to her views, I am not certain . . . I do not know, Georgiana. I do so wish that I did. But it is a possibility. Would you wish me well in that direction?"

He recalled his surprise when she at first made no reply, but instead came across the room and took his hand, and then said,

"There is nothing I would like better. But do not worry, I shall keep your secret, whatever happens."

Perhaps Georgiana would be more than the young sister he needed to protect from now on. Someone who would be close both to himself and to Elizabeth. Darcy drew up a chair to the desk, took paper and pen, and began to write. The clock in his room had struck the hour before he concluded the letter,

> . . . I hope, therefore, my dear sister, that you will wish us both well, and happy.
>
> Should you hear from our aunt in Kent, do not be surprised if Lady Catherine takes a different view. I shall also be writing to her.
>
> I will send this to Pemberley by the post tomorrow,

and will write again, as soon as there is more news to tell.

    Your affectionate brother,
    Fitzwilliam Darcy.

The following day, Mr. Bennet had made the announcement to the rest of his family before Darcy arrived with Bingley at Longbourn, and he and Elizabeth were the centre of many happy congratulations.

Mrs. Bennet appeared to be so in awe of her intended son-in-law, that she ventured not to speak to him, unless she was able to offer him some attention, or mark her deference for his opinion. She confined her conversation to such queries as "Tell me, Mr. Darcy, what dish you are particularly fond of, so that we may have it this evening?"

Soon after their arrival, his host took him aside into his study.

"I understand from Lizzy that you took the major part, Sir, in bringing about the marriage between my youngest daughter, Lydia, and that fellow Wickham. I am most exceedingly obliged to you for your trouble. You must let me repay you, as soon as maybe."

Darcy had given some thought to how he should reply to this request, should it arise. He had concluded overnight that it would give him the best opportunity of convincing Mr. Bennet of his real attachment to Elizabeth, of which her father had seemed to be in some doubt on the previous day.

"I have, as I believe you know, Sir, more than sufficient means, so that the expenditure is of little concern to me. But even if I had been in a different situation, I would have done every thing just the same, for Elizabeth's peace of mind. In all that I had to do, to bring the marriage about, she was always in my thoughts. I did nothing without her being foremost in my mind. And without her beside me, there can be no happiness for me in the future. So let there be no more talk of repayment, I beg of you. Your consent to our marriage is more than enough compensation for me."

Mr. Bennet had never appeared to Darcy to be a man lost for words, but this seemed almost to leave him without speech.

When he did recover, it was to say, quite simply, "Jane is a good girl, but Lizzy is my favourite child of all my daughters. Without her I shall have little comfort here. I hope that you will not object if I visit her at Pemberley, especially when Mrs. Bennet is busy elsewhere, perhaps a little more often than I ought."

Darcy replied, "I shall be happy to shake your hand on that."

Later that morning, Bingley agreed that his carriage should be sent to Longbourn on the next day, so that Miss Bennet and her sister could take luncheon at Netherfield. It was arranged that Mary Bennet should accompany them, as Bingley had made her the offer of playing on the piano-forte, which she had last seen on the night of the Netherfield ball the previous November.

When Elizabeth and her sisters arrived at Netherfield on the next morning, this occupation soon took Mary away from the rest of the party, and Bingley and Jane went off with the housekeeper to discuss the decoration of the rooms to her taste prior to their wedding.

Darcy and Elizabeth made their way to the drawing-room, where he took the first opportunity of asking what Mr. Bennet's reaction had been when she spoke to her father about their marriage.

Elizabeth gave him that lively smile that was sure to set Darcy's heart racing, as she said,

"I told him that you have no improper pride—that you are perfectly amiable. I assured him that you really were the object of my choice, and explained the gradual change which my estimation of you had undergone. I told him that I was certain that your affection for me was not the work of a day, but had stood the test of many months' suspense."

Elizabeth added, with an even more mischievous smile, "And, of course, I enumerated all your good qualities, and finally convinced him that we should be the happiest couple in the world!"

It was with some difficulty, at the end of this recital, that Darcy retained the measure of composure appropriate to his situation in the company of an unmarried lady without any chaperone on hand.

"And did you," he said, to steady himself, and seeking to echo her own bantering tone, "tell him that you cared a little for me?"

"Yes, I did," she replied and, in a much more sober manner as she turned to face him directly, she said, "and I do, though not a little, as I hope you know by now."

37

The next day, at Longbourn, Elizabeth and Darcy sat by the window at the far end of the parlour, and she asked him to account for his having ever fallen in love with her.

"How could you begin?" said she. "I can comprehend your going on charmingly, when you had once made a beginning; but what could set you off in the first place?"

Darcy was already discovering that he had difficulty in maintaining a proper decorum when she addressed him in this playful fashion, but it was perhaps a question deserving a serious answer.

"I cannot fix on the hour, or the spot, or the look, or the words, which laid the foundation. It is too long ago. I was in the middle before I knew that I had begun."

But it seemed that she was determined to make him smile.

"My beauty you had early withstood, and as for my manners, my behaviour to you was at least always bordering on the uncivil, and I never spoke to you without rather wishing to give you pain than not. Now be sincere; did you admire me for my impertinence?"

He had to succumb at this, and laughed with her as he said, "For the liveliness of your mind, I did."

"You may as well call it impertinence at once. It was very little less."

Elizabeth then took a more serious tone, as she continued.

"The fact is, that you were sick of civility, of defence, of officious attention. You were disgusted with the women who were always speaking and looking, and thinking for your approbation alone. I roused, and interested you, because I was so unlike them. Had you not been really amiable you would have hated me for it; but in spite of the pains you took to disguise yourself, your feelings were always noble and just; and in your heart, you thoroughly despised the persons who so assiduously courted you."

He refused to be provoked into agreeing with her.

"There, I have saved you the trouble of accounting for it; and really, all things considered, I begin to think it perfectly reasonable. To be sure, you knew no actual good of me, but nobody thinks of that when they fall in love."

"Was there no good in your affectionate behaviour to Jane, while she was ill here at Netherfield?"

"Dearest Jane! Who could have done less for her? But make a virtue of it by all means. My good qualities are under your protection, and you are to exaggerate them as much as possible; and, in return, it belongs to me to find occasions for teasing and quarrelling with you as often as may be."

She smiled bewitchingly, and then was suddenly more

serious as she said, "I shall begin directly by asking you what made you so unwilling to come to the point at last. What made you so shy of me, when you first called, and afterwards dined at Longbourn? Why, especially, when you called, did you look as if you did not care about me?"

"Because you were grave and silent, and gave me no encouragement."

"But I was embarrassed."

"And so was I."

"You might have talked to me more when you came to dinner."

"A man who had felt less, might."

"How unlucky that you should have a reasonable answer to give, and that I should be so reasonable as to admit it! But I wonder how long you would have gone on, if you had been left to yourself. I wonder when you would have spoken, if I had not asked you! My resolution of thanking you for your kindness to Lydia had certainly great effect. Too much, I am afraid; for what becomes of the moral, if our comfort springs from a breach of promise, for I ought not to have mentioned the subject? This will never do."

"You need not distress yourself," said Darcy. "The moral will be perfectly fair. Lady Catherine's unjustifiable endeavours to separate us, were the means of removing all my doubts. I am not indebted for my present happiness to your eager desire of expressing your gratitude. I was not in a humour to wait for any opening of yours. My aunt's intelligence had given me hope, and I was determined at once to know every thing."

"Lady Catherine has been of infinite use, which ought to make her happy, for she loves to be of use. But tell me, what did you come down to Netherfield for? Was it merely to ride to Longbourn and be embarrassed? Or had you intended any more serious consequence?"

"My real purpose was to see you, and to judge, if I could, whether I might ever hope to make you love me. My avowed one, or what I avowed to myself, was to see whether your sister was still partial to Bingley, and if she were, to make the confession to him which I have since made."

"Shall you ever have courage to announce to Lady Catherine, what is to befall her?"

"I am more likely to want time than courage, Elizabeth. But it ought to be done, and if you will give me a sheet of paper, it shall be done directly."

"And if I had not a letter to write myself, I might sit by you, and admire the evenness of your writing, as another young lady once did. But I have an aunt, too, who must not be longer neglected."

For above a quarter of an hour, there was a companionable silence in the room as they pursued their correspondence. Darcy finished his letter long before Elizabeth completed hers, and sat quietly, secure in the pleasure of watching her. Slowly, she became aware of his attention, and turned to smile a little.

"Before I seal the letter," Elizabeth said, "may I add an invitation for my aunt and uncle to stay with us at Pemberley — I know that my aunt especially would welcome that."

"By all means," he said. "We are, you know, to be wed soon after the end of November. Would you like to ask them to join us, with their children, for the Christmas festival?"

He needed no more answer than the wonderful smile which came over her face.

"But," Darcy added in a tone that attempted to sound sombre, "there is one condition!"

Elizabeth looked at him a little warily. "And, pray, Sir, what is that?"

"I recall that there is a young lady with whom I first disdained to dance who, on other occasions, twice refused my invitation to do so, including once to dance a reel of which her elder sister has since told me she is very fond. Then when at last she did dance with me at Netherfield, I recall that she insisted on advocating the claims and qualities of a certain Mr. Wickham, and trying to establish my own character."

She looked somewhat embarrassed at this, and even rather apprehensive.

Seeing her expression, Darcy could maintain his assumed severity no longer.

"All I mean to ask you is whether you will join with me to hold a ball for our neighbours at Pemberley on New Year's Eve. It was a happy custom of my parents to entertain their friends from the county on that day—a custom which ceased on my mother's death."

He was silent for a few moments as he said that, and then recollected himself, and gave her a teasing smile.

"Then," he continued, "you could not escape the opening of the first dance with me, and the occasion would give me the opportunity to introduce you to some of our Derbyshire neighbours. As Bingley and Jane are to spend Christmas in Hertfordshire, visiting your family at Longbourn, they could travel up in time to join us. And perhaps my cousin Fitzwilliam also?"

And so it was settled, and the arrangements put in hand.

38

Georgiana wasted no time in replying to her brother's letter. The joy which she expressed on receiving the news of their forthcoming wedding was so great that four sides of paper were insufficient to contain all her delight.

On the same day as her letter was received, the family at Longbourn heard that unexpected visitors were suddenly come from Hunsford to Lucas Lodge—Mr. and Mrs. Collins.

The news from Mrs. Collins that his aunt had been rendered exceedingly angry by the contents of her nephew's letter did not trouble Darcy. Elizabeth soon heard from Charlotte that, although herself very happy about the match, she had decided that it would be very wise for them both to get away from Kent for a time. The reason for the Collinses' arrival was soon confirmed by a letter for Darcy, which arrived from Lady Catherine by the next post. It was angry and abusive of Elizabeth to the highest degree, and he resolved to send no reply.

Darcy could see that the arrival of her friend was a sincere pleasure to Elizabeth, though having Mr. Collins parading and addressing Darcy with obsequious civility was a trial which the latter did his best, for Elizabeth's sake, to bear calmly.

He found Mr. Collins no more wearing than Sir William Lucas, who complimented him on carrying away the brightest jewel in the country every time they met, and expressed his hopes of their all meeting frequently at St. James's. Elizabeth's aunt in Meryton, Mrs. Philips, was a greater tax on his forbearance. Though she regarded Darcy with too much awe to speak with the familiarity which his friend Bingley's good humour encouraged, yet, whenever she did speak, she must be vulgar.

Elizabeth did all she could to shield him from these embarrassments, and was anxious to keep him to herself, and together with those of her family with whom he might converse without mortification.

However, Darcy was aware that her concern about the uncomfortable feelings of all this took away for her from what should have been the pleasures of courtship. They both looked forward to the time when they should be together at Pemberley.

Matters continued in this fashion until, one morning a few days later, and about six weeks before their wedding, Elizabeth came to him.

She spoke rather hesitantly.

"My father tells me, Sir, that you are intending to make a most generous settlement on me on the occasion of our marriage."

"My dear, it is no more than you deserve, or than I would wish for your comfort and security," he replied, taking her hand.

And then an idea came to him. He wished nothing more than to be in her company every day, and a few days away from Hertfordshire would not be unwelcome.

"Elizabeth, it is several weeks since I saw Georgiana, and she is still in Derbyshire. She will, of course, be at our wedding. But a thought occurs to me. I must instruct my attorney to draw up your settlement, and your father says that Mr. Phillips can act for him on your behalf.

"However, rather than my travelling to town alone, Mr. Bennet could use your uncle Gardiner's man in London, who was of great assistance to us in the matter of Lydia and Wickham. Would you be willing to accompany your father, if he is agreeable, to be in town for a few days, whilst these matters are settled? If so, I could write to Georgiana, and she could join me from Pemberley. Would the Gardiners be willing to receive you? I could then also show you our house in London."

The manner of her reply left him in no doubt.

"Oh yes, Sir! And I am sure that my father would be very happy to be away from Longbourn, and all my mother's preparations—although no doubt she will have some commissions for both of us to execute whilst we are in town."

As Elizabeth had anticipated, her father greeted the suggestion with what in him amounted to alacrity, and the course of a few days brought happy confirmation of the welcome awaiting Elizabeth and her father in Gracechurch Street.

Darcy at the same time sent word to Derbyshire, and Georgiana confirmed that she and Mrs. Annesley could be in town within the week.

39

It was a happy reunion for Darcy and Elizabeth with her uncle and his family when the coach called at the Gardiners' home to deliver Mr. Bennet and his daughter for their stay in town.

Georgiana was expected in London the same day. It was arranged that Mr. Bennet and Darcy should meet with the attorneys on the morrow, and that Georgiana should then go with them to the Gardiners' home for luncheon.

His sister's meeting with Elizabeth was all that Darcy had hoped. It was clear that they would become more than the best of friends, and the two young ladies were soon in earnest conversation about the commissions which Mrs. Bennet had given on Jane's behalf, for various furnishings were needed at Netherfield.

Mrs. Gardiner undertook to direct her brother and her niece to the nearest warehouses to choose samples for despatch to Hertfordshire, and it was agreed that Mr. Bennet and Elizabeth should then go to Darcy's house for the rest of the day.

Mrs. Bennet's requests having been dealt with, Darcy and his sister welcomed Elizabeth and her father on their arrival. Mr. Bennet was quick to accept Georgiana's invitation to view the library.

"It is much less, Sir, than I have at Pemberley, but you may find something of interest," Darcy observed, as Mr. Bennet and Georgiana left the drawing-room.

"Where would you like to go first?" he asked, turning to Elizabeth.

"There is something I would like to ask you, before we go round the house," she replied, "if I may. It concerns Charlotte. It may be difficult, at least for a while, for us to visit Rosings, and you would not want me to stay at the parsonage at Hunsford. Neither of us would seek out Mr. Collins' company, I know, but she was—indeed still is—a dear friend of mine. Would you object if, from time to time, she called in to see me here on her way to her family in Hertfordshire? She told me that she carried a message to you from Lady Catherine earlier this year."

"Yes, indeed. She warned me of the reason for Lady Catherine planning a visit to town, and I was most grateful to be able to escape to Essex, to see my cousin, as a result!" said Darcy with feeling. "You are welcome to invite her to stay overnight here at any time, just so long as we can always be certain that Mr. Collins will be detained in Kent and unable to come with her!"

She thanked him warmly.

He turned as though to show her the room, but then

stopped, and said, rather urgently, "Tell me, my dear, there is something that your sister Kitty mentioned to me last week at Longbourn that puzzled me, concerning Mr. Collins . . . about my being your second proposal."

"Kitty ought not to have mentioned that. Although it was absurd as far as I was concerned, Mr. Collins did make an offer for my hand shortly after the ball at Netherfield. He had good intentions, at least in part, so that the entail giving Longbourn to him after my father's death should not wholly disadvantage the rest of my family."

Then she added, in a more lively tone,

"So, you see, I might have been subject to a daily sermon, not to mention a regular discourse on the state of Mr. Collins' cabbages, such as my dear friend Charlotte has to bear. That would have been a heavy burden indeed, would it not?"

And she turned back with a quick smile to look at Darcy, until she saw his expression.

"Why, Sir, what is the matter?"

Darcy's emotion at hearing her reply was so strong that he had to struggle to compose himself before he answered. Then he spoke vehemently, and with much less delicacy than perhaps was appropriate.

"It is the thought of Mr. Collins and you . . . of him having the right to . . . No, it does not bear thinking about!"

Elizabeth's response to this was first to blush deeply, as she understood the meaning of his words. Then, after a short pause, she came forward and took his hands in hers.

It was several minutes before Darcy said,

"Where can your father be? Georgiana must be a very

eloquent guide to the library, for they have been gone at least a half hour!"

"I had not noticed . . . ," she paused, and coloured again as she said, "shall we go to them now?"

"In a moment," Darcy said, "but first there is something you should see upstairs," and he led the way to a sitting-room on the first floor overlooking the square. The furnishings were pleasant, if faded.

"This was my mother's, and is as she left it."

Elizabeth looked around her. "It must have many memories for you," she said, looking at him keenly.

"Yes. But happy ones. I would like you to use it, if you will, and change the furnishings to your taste."

"You were very fond of your mother?"

"Yes. She was," he smiled, "a strong character, but a less dominating person than her elder sister, Lady Catherine. I wish that she had known you."

"And I her. I will be very happy to have her room."

~ 40 ~

The legal agreements having been settled, the marriages between Bingley and Miss Jane Bennet, and between Darcy and his dearest Elizabeth, took place as planned and, within a few days, Mr. and Mrs. Darcy were in Derbyshire.

The weather was fine for the time of year, and Darcy took great pleasure in showing Elizabeth the house, and the many walks and drives round the estate. The path alongside the stream that they had taken with her uncle and aunt a few months earlier had special memories for both. Darcy was also able to take his bride on the drive together in the curricle around the park that they had been denied by Lydia Bennet's elopement.

He could not remember a happier time for him at Pemberley, and told Elizabeth so.

Shortly before Christmas, they were joined by Georgiana, and by Mr. and Mrs. Gardiner together with their children, and the festive season was celebrated with a pleasant informality and much laughter. Darcy caused Elizabeth to blush in front of the family by teasing her that, soon, the childish voices in the house might not be only those of welcome guests. She replied quietly but with a lively smile that she admitted that could be a possibility, should that be his preference.

Darcy took pleasure in seeing the ease with which his bride began to settle to the ways of running Pemberley. The preparations were already under way for the ball to be held on the eve of the New Year, and Georgiana delighted in showing her new sister all the corners of the house. Together, she and Elizabeth oversaw the details of the repast to be prepared. The day before the ball, Bingley and Jane arrived from Hertfordshire and, with Darcy's cousin Fitzwilliam, joined the family already assembled.

It was with great pleasure on the eve of the New Year that Darcy welcomed his neighbours and introduced them to Elizabeth. When the time came, they took to the floor together to open the dancing.

As the music began, she turned to him in surprise, and said, "Is this not the same tune as was played at the ball at Netherfield last year? And, the same dance as we took together?"

"But of course!" said Darcy, smiling at her. "There was nothing the matter with either, all that was needed was for us to come to a proper understanding."

And thus it was that, surrounded by their friends from Derbyshire and the relatives most dear to them, Mr. and Mrs. Fitzwilliam Darcy began their life together, in the comfort and elegance of their family party at Pemberley.

THE HISTORY

BEHIND

THE STORY

The Author, Janet Aylmer, Talks About Writing Darcy's Story

Since *Pride and Prejudice* was first published nearly 200 years ago, it has become one of the best-loved novels in the English Language. Like many other people, I first read the book whilst I was at school, as did my children, and have enjoyed reading the novel again many times since then.

Modern media—radio, the cinema and television—have introduced *Pride and Prejudice* to many new audiences all around the world in recent years. It was after watching the BBC television serial in 1995, and discussing it with one of my daughters, that my curiosity was re-awakened about Mr. Darcy, and I decided to write this book for her. That led to the idea that other people might also enjoy reading *Darcy's Story*.

I have been surprised and delighted to discover that my need to know more about Jane Austen's hero is shared by people all over the world. At the time of writing, the book has been sold to readers not only in Great Britain, but in 37 other countries around the world via the Internet. Over 20,000 copies of the book have now been sold. The publishers have received many letters and emails expressing the enjoyment that so many people have found in reading *Darcy's Story*. It seems that complementing *Pride and Prejudice* by writing this book has satisfied a long-felt need for many readers.

Everyone who has ever read Jane Austen's novel will have their own idea of Mr. Darcy's side of the story, and this book could be described as looking through the mirror of *Pride and Prejudice* (1940) from the other side. I am delighted that a story written nearly 200 years ago can still give pleasure in a very different era. I have also been glad to learn that people much more knowledgeable than I am about Jane Austen and her work have also liked the book.

I saw the cinema film of "Pride and Prejudice" some years ago and can remember being very disappointed that the story was changed at the end. That seemed to me to distort the story as told by Jane Austen. So I started by making a conscious that the book must be totally faithful to *Pride and Prejudice* and not change that story at all. Jane Austen wrote her novel very much from the point of view of the heroine, Elizabeth Bennet, and her family, and tells us very little about his side of the story. We learn a great deal about Elizabeth Bennet, her four sisters, and their family life.

I looked very carefully at what the chronological sequence of events was in *Pride and Prejudice* and, almost as important, what Darcy would not have known about the story as told by Jane Austen. Her novel covers a period lasting from the autumn of the first year to the winter of the second.

Wickham's attempt to elope with Darcy's sister, Georgiana, had taken place before he met Elizabeth Bennet, although in *Pride and Prejudice* Darcy tells her about it in the letter after his proposal at the following Easter. So, in *Darcy's Story*, Wickham's visit to Ramsgate to persuade Georgiana to elope with him comes near the beginning of the book.

Mr. Darcy is only "present" in *Pride and Prejudice* for a few weeks at Netherfield (his friend Bingley's house) in the first autumn; for two to three weeks at his aunt Lady Catherine de Bourgh's house in Kent the following Easter; for a few days in Derbyshire in the summer; and then at the end of the story when he meets Elizabeth Bennet again in Hertfordshire. So *Darcy's Story* has to explain what happened before he went to Netherfield, whether it was just chance that he met Elizabeth Bennet again in Kent, and at last in Hertfordshire, and what happened in between.

He did not visit Longbourn, the Bennets' home, until close to the end of *Pride and Prejudice*. He knew nothing of the proposal of marriage made by the curate Mr. Collins to his cousin Elizabeth shortly after the Netherfield ball, which she had rejected with her father's support, but against her mother's wishes.

Although he had a poor opinion of some other members of her family, Darcy respected Jane Bennet, and was aware of the close bond between Elizabeth and her elder sister.

His actions in *Pride and Prejudice* confirmed that he was a very fond and protective brother to his own sister Georgiana. Darcy seemed to me to be someone who was still brooding over the early death of his mother, of whom he had been very fond. Having suffered the early deaths of both his own parents, it may be that he envied Elizabeth having the close family that he himself had lost.

A major decision was how much of Jane Austen's conversation between Darcy and Elizabeth Bennet to use. She wrote much of *Pride and Prejudice* in a lively and ironic style, which suited Elizabeth's character and was appropriate, as that story is told from the heroine's point of view.

Either Jane Austen's dialogue had to be changed into description only, or there needed to be some form of commentary to show that Darcy had a very different view of the situations and their conversations when he and Elizabeth were both present. I decided that the story would be more enjoyable if I used the second approach, even though that meant repeating some lengthy sections of dialogue which Jane wrote. What I could not do was use different words between them for the conversations which Jane Austen herself had "reported!"

Jane Austen made it clear that Elizabeth's parents were not well matched, and Mr. Bennet confirms this when he seeks to dissuade her from marrying Darcy if she cannot respect her "partner in life."

Darcy was a very different character from Elizabeth, more sombre and reserved, perhaps because he had become used to keeping his own counsel, and not sharing his emotions. It therefore seemed wrong to use the much lighter style writing employed to such brilliant effect in *Pride and Prejudice*.

I am sure that everyone who has read and enjoyed Jane Austen's novel has their own particular favourite passages in the book, and I used many of mine in *Darcy's Story*. As her novel was first published in several "parts," I also used quotations from *Pride and Prejudice* to introduce each of the seven parts in my book.

Having Darcy recall past conversations was one way to show the more serious and reflective aspects of his character, and emphasise passages from Jane Austen's novel which are especially relevant to *Darcy's Story*.

Jane Austen described her hero at the beginning of *Pride and Prejudice* as being a wealthy but proud young man who moved only in the most elevated circles. Wealth and an emphasis on social class had been paramount in his upbringing.

As he said in *Pride and Prejudice*, "As a child I was taught what was right, but I was not taught to correct my temper. I was given good principles, but left to follow them in pride and conceit. . . . I was spoilt by my parents, who . . . allowed, encouraged, almost taught me to be selfish and overbearing, to care for none beyond my own family circle, to think meanly of all the rest of the world, to wish at least to think meanly of their sense and worth compared with my own."

Although Darcy came from a grander and wealthier background than Elizabeth Bennet, she was more able to cope with, and was more confident in, new social situations than he was. I saw Darcy as someone who could only enjoy life with someone very different from the superior and over-confident females, such as Caroline Bingley, whom he finds intimidating and superficial.

The Bingley sisters were fixed in their views, with a critical and derogatory approach to anyone who did not move in their own "circle." Only Darcy's friend, their brother Charles, took people as he found them, perhaps remembering how his family's fortune had been made in trade.

I felt that Darcy seemed to be one person at the beginning of *Pride and Prejudice*, and quite another at the end. People do not really change that much, so it was more likely that he had been acting a part to some extent, concealing some inhibition or aspect of his real character.

Jane Austen had Darcy say in her novel that ". . . . I cannot forget the follies and vices of others so soon as I ought, nor their offences against myself . . . My temper would perhaps be called resentful. My good opinion once lost is lost for ever." His wariness of Mr. Wickham, son of his late father's steward, was confirmed by Wickham's attempts to get more than he was due from Darcy's father's estate. That wariness had developed into dislike and distrust before Wickham tried to elope with Darcy's younger sister, Georgiana, to get control of her fortune.

Darcy's disdain for the Court at St. James and his dislike of mixing with people strange to him seemed to be due to the fact that he was not at ease in unfamiliar company, and envied other young men's ability to converse with and charm the opposite sex, rather than that he was naturally unpleasant to other people.

I took this as my cue, that he was envious of the easy manners of many of the people he knew, especially the men of about his own age such as Wickham, his cousin Fitzwilliam, and his friend Bingley.

Darcy seemed to me to be a strong person. He could take swift action when he chose, as when he resolved the elopement of Elizabeth's sister Lydia with Wickham.

Jane Austen herself describes Darcy as being a good brother to Georgiana, as being at ease with people he knows well, and as being generous to the poor in Derbyshire. If you like, his unattractive manners in the earlier part of the story concealed a very pleasant character waiting to emerge, if the right person came along to help him escape his haughty relations and gain confidence that he could find the happiness he sought in marriage.

I decided that Darcy was unlikely to have reacted favourably to the news that Elizabeth might have married Mr. Collins, since Jane Austen made it clear that they had very little in common except for Darcy's formidable aunt, Lady Catherine De Bourgh.

But he was likely to learn about that proposal, sooner or later, from someone in the Bennet family who was aware of it. But Mr. Collins did do Darcy an unintentional favour, by telling his aunt about the impending marriage between Jane Bennet and Mr. Bingley. His concern that a union between her nephew and Elizabeth might follow led her to her famous interview with Elizabeth at Longbourn, and her subsequent visit to London to try and dissuade Darcy from the idea.

Every novel has a turning point, and *Darcy's Story* is no exception. Darcy's sister Georgiana seemed to me to have reached marriageable age in a story set in the 19th century, as had Elizabeth's youngest sister Lydia. Georgiana was therefore at the point when she was changing from being Darcy's responsibility to becoming more his contemporary. So talking to Georgiana about his troubled frame of mind, after his first unsuccessful proposal to Elizabeth, fitted the story, and I made that the turning point in Darcy's "journey" to win the hand of the woman he loves.

The lighter side of
HISTORY

✱ Look for this seal on select historical fiction titles from Harper. Books bearing it contain special bonus materials, including timelines, interviews with the author, insights into the real-life events that inspired the book, as well as recommendations for further reading.

THORNFIELD HALL
Jane Eyre's Hidden Story
by Emma Tennant

ISBN 0-06-000455-X (paperback)

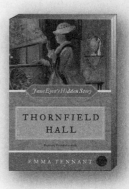

Adèle is a homesick, forlorn eight-year-old when first brought to Thornfield Hall by her mother's former lover. She longs to return to the glitter of Paris—and to the mother who has been lost to her. But a small ray of sunshine brightens her eternal gloom when a stranger arrives to care for her: a serious yet intensely loving young governess named Jane Eyre.

"Tennant's story works perfectly, creating a genuine modern sequel to Bronte's tale." —*Kirkus Reviews*

REBECCA
by Daphne Du Maurier

ISBN 0-380-73040-5 (paperback)

"Last night I dreamt I went to Manderley again . . ." With these words the reader is ushered into an isolated gray stone manse on the windswept Cornish coast, as the second Mrs. Maxim de Winter recalls the chilling events that transpired as she began her new life as the young bride of a husband she barely knew.

REBECCA'S TALE
by Sally Beauman

ISBN 0-06-117467-X (paperback)

"If you've read *Rebecca* and loved it, Beauman brings it to more colorful life." —*Chicago Tribune*

"What a savory treat—a mixture of mystery and romance flavored with intelligence, compassion, and wit."
—Sena Jeter Naslund, author of *Ahab's Wife*

THE WIDOW'S WAR
A Novel
by Sally Gunning

ISBN 0-06-079158-6 (paperback)

"Skillfully employing the language, imagination, and character that literary fiction demands, [Gunning] illuminates a fascinating moment in our past."
—Anita Shreve, *Washington Post Book World*

THE FAMILY FORTUNE
A Modern Retelling of Jane Austen's *Persuasion*

by Laurie Horowitz

ISBN 0-06-087527-5 (paperback)

"Horowitz has finely captured the bored silliness of WASP high society, creating a stylish portrait of an endangered species." —*Kirkus Reviews*

"Rich with divinely dysfunctional contemporary characters who could have stepped from a Jane Austen novel."
—Mary Kay Andrews, bestselling author of *Savannah Breeze*

AND ONLY TO DECEIVE
A Novel of Suspense
by Tasha Alexander

ISBN 0-06-114844-X (paperback)

"Charming." —*Publishers Weekly*

"This engaging, witty mix of Victorian cozy and suspense thriller draws its dramatic spark from the endearingly headstrong heroine's growth in life and love. A memorable debut." —*Booklist*

TO THE TOWER BORN
A Novel of the Lost Princes
by Robin Maxwell

ISBN 0-06-058052-6 (paperback)

"As she did in *The Wild Irish*, Maxwell once again delivers a fresh take on an old story, giving the world a new theory to debate." —*Library Journal*

DARCY'S STORY
Pride and Prejudice Told From a Whole New Perspective
by Janet Aylmer

ISBN 0-06-114870-9 (paperback)

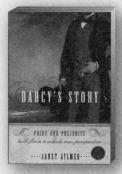

Janet Aylmer has cleverly re-written a beloved classic from a different point of view. Initially seen by Elizabeth as "haughty, reserved and fastidious," Aylmer's story explains the underlying thoughts, feelings, and motivations behind Mr. Darcy's cold exterior.

THE FOOL'S TALE
A Novel
by Nicole Galland

ISBN 0-06-072151-0 (paperback)

"Set in an age when marriage was strategy, love was temptation, and treachery was a tool of survival, Nicole Galland's *The Fool's Tale* creates a vivid 12th-century world and three unforgettable characters."
—William Dietrich, author of *Hadrian's Wall*

THE CANTERBURY PAPERS
A Novel
by Judith Healey

ISBN 0-06-077332-4 (paperback)

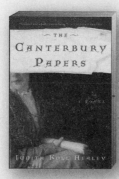

"[An] engaging medieval suspense debut. . . . Healey's well-researched historical drama . . . delights in poking fun at the stuffiness and misbehavior that characterized the royal families of the time. . . . Fresh and absorbing." —*Publishers Weekly*